SPEAKING TO THE ROSE

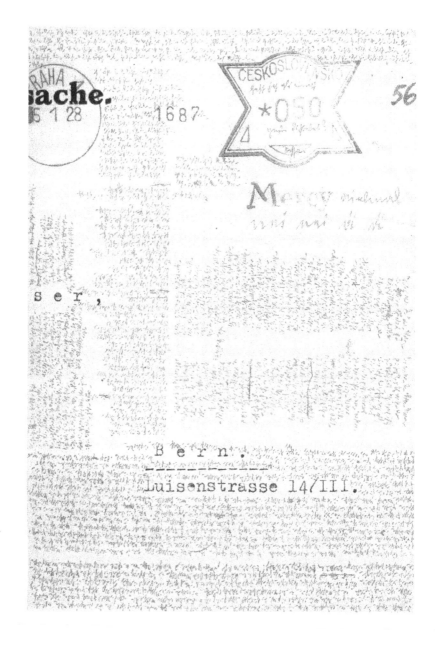

"Aus dem Bleistiftgebeit," No. 566: original size.

Robert Walser

Speaking to the Rose

WRITINGS, 1912-1932

Selected and
Translated by

Christopher
Middleton

UNIVERSITY OF
NEBRASKA PRESS
LINCOLN & LONDON

Publication of this book was assisted by a grant from the National Endowment for the Arts.

License edition and reproduction of microscripts by permission of the owner of rights, the Carl-Seelig-Stiftung, Zürich © Suhrkamp Verlag 1986

Library of Congress Cataloging-in-Publication Data

Walser, Robert, 1878–1956.

[Short stories. English. Selections.] Speaking to the rose : writings, 1912–1932 / Robert Walser; selected and translated by Christopher Middleton.

p.   cm.   ISBN 0-8032-4807-5 (cloth : alk. paper)—ISBN 0-8032-9833-1 (pbk. : alk. paper)

1. Walser, Robert, 1878–1956—Translations into English. I. Middleton, Christopher, 1926– II. Title.

PT2647.A64A25 2005

833'.912—dc22

2005041793

CONTENTS

PREFACE

The two earlier books of translations from Robert Walser, *Selected Stories* (1983) and *Masquerade* (1990), were drawn largely from Walser's eight collections of short prose texts published between 1904 and 1925. There were, however, in both earlier selections texts drawn from work not collected or published during Walser's lifetime. The present selection includes only two translations from his books. All else is drawn from that uncollected work, except for fourteen translations from what has come to be called the "pencil area," or "Bleistiftgebiet."

The "pencil area" was for a long time thought to be a *corpus hermeticum*, closed to the mortal mind because composed in an entirely private cipher. It was by matching certain strips of script to extant published texts that Jochen Greven first showed that the cipher had been all along an adroitly, if most idiosyncratically, abbreviated script. The 526 packages of this writing now fill 2,000 pages in the six volumes of *Aus dem Bleistiftgebiet*, 1985–2000, edited by the meticulous decipherers Bernard Echte and Werner Morlang. So here was a real *trouvaille*: sometime even before 1924 or 1925, Walser had begun to pencil, on the backs of calendars, on blank spaces offered by rejection slips, telegrams, bank statements, and other sorts of used stationery, an immense reserve of stories, feuilletons, sketches, improvisations, from which to extract, at will, fair copies. To make this new selection I then relied on volumes numbered 15–20 in the collected works (*Sämtliche Werke in einzelnen Bänden*, 1966–), and on those faithfully deciphered multifarious "calligraphic" pencil microscripts.

The date at the end of each text is that of first publication or of writing: of the former when a source is spelled out, of the latter when followed by *SW* (for *Sämtliche Werke*). Some notes, a chronology of Walser's life and work, and details of prior translations appear at the end of the book.

The chronological sequence of the texts should not be mistaken for a means to focus attention on Walser as a person. As author and individual, Walser articulates a large and general cast of mind, such as strictly "personal" writings seldom do. He can be considered a voice of the unvanquished downtrodden (in early work, of the employee), of people never quite small enough to slip through power's mesh, of the powerless who do not squirm but resist. Elusive as he is, his mimicries, his discontinuous digressions, ironies, even simulations, project an authentic and vital type, *homo ludens*, for whom creative play is the desirable thing, even the sublime thing. His prose, more agile than proper, more obstinately naif than burnished, certainly has ancestors, but it stands apart from other literary registers (as does that of Joyce or of Beckett). This otherness may be Swiss: that Walser spoke Swiss-German his prose does remind us. Yet he also did maintain a stand, seldom without his slingshot, in opposition to the grander writing in German of his time.

Through the 1960s, most of Walser's new admirers were apt to detect in his writings one single main (if secret) motif, such as Angst (Elias Canetti), Irony (Martin Walser), or else a type of folk trickster's Buffoonery. Spread the twenty volumes and the six of microscripts now before you, and such divinations are thrown in doubt. There are, for instance, several later straight texts about Jesus and his family, which cannot possi-

für den Beitrag *m* BERLINER TAGEBLATT No 220

Hochachtend

Honorar-Verrechnungsstelle

bly be construed in the ironic voice audible in "The Cave Man" ("We are workers, Christians"). In the microscripts we can even discover Walser taking a positive shine to Catherine of Siena. No doubt his running contest with polymorphous selfhood finds a paradigm in worldwide religious exhortation to purge the soul of its deluded, layered, infernal self-will and unite it in charity with universal Spirit. Some of Walser's foibles might even have made him, in certain moods, a moderate Tolstoyan. But the selection I have made (not least for the pleasure of translation) does not in any way legitimize a religious, let alone "Christian," reading of the entire work. To confine Walser, to locate his work, in any system of beliefs, or in any pathology (however generalized), can only be a most grudging response to the sensibility of such a wild particle.

The owl of Minerva flies, Hegel thought, at nightfall. Under Minerva's tutelage Walser certainly was not. Yet there is an owlishness about his narrative gaze. While forging on with these new translations I have often been made aware of a daimon of owlishness exposing Walser at a curious angle to the European culture he had at his fingertips, while his spirited address to all existence had to meet, head-on, the catastrophic darkening of his times, their pivot being the First World War. Europe became a theme he flexes every which way, its chivalric past, the puny ceremonies of its present. And it is no small irony that such an enchanting disenchanter should write in 1927: "In my opinion a writer who means to some extent well by his fellow beings should, if he can, so conduct himself as to help to save the illusions and protect them from being supplanted by illusionlessness."

The qualification "to some extent" surely touches with ambiguity the rest of the statement. To save the illusions: yet was the "pencil area"—as Werner Morlang has wryly suggested—"a total work of art in a nutshell"? The fourteen texts translated allow no more than glimpses of the whole fabric. And there it is, cryptically inscribed on ruins of paper, as if broken columns became trees again, and akin to Monsú Desiderio's seventeenth-century illusionary canvases of vast crumbling towers and palaces, a cosmos in fragmentation, the haunt (as William Gaunt wrote of Desiderio) of "a lunar spirit which led to the construction of dead cities and disquieting arcades of fancy."

Even so, there is a caveat to be observed: the reader must bear it in mind that the *B* texts are the outcome of judicious and gradual deciphering, but not texts that Walser himself pruned, polished, and proofread. We must devoutly allow for a difference in kind, and as regards internal consistency, between microscript and finished work. The translations pass over only a few and not substantial doubts as to the transcription (such as are editorially indicated in the source).

I have closed the selection with one of Walser's later poems. Is the lady wearing long gloves an uncaring Muse? Is this an anima figure, miffed at being dressed up? Asked for his opinion, Jochen Greven replied: "For me this lady personifies not so much a Muse as the fatality latent in social validation. Or else she is the twin sister to the hope, to the anticipatory joy that lives in the heart—Melancholia, terrifying and paralyzing depression, possibly with the overpowering features of a raging mother . . . " Might it be that at rock-bottom Walser could release his deepest spring?

C. M.

SPEAKING TO THE ROSE

A Note on Van Gogh's L'Arlésienne

In front of this picture one has all kinds of thoughts, and to someone absorbed in it many questions occur, questions at once so simple and so strange and so disconcerting that they seem to be unanswerable. In the picture, many questions find their finest, most subtle, most delicate significance—which is that they cannot be answered. When, for instance, a lover asks his lady, "Can I still have hopes?" and she doesn't answer, then this absence of an answer sometimes signifies a heavenly Yes. That is how it is with everything that puzzles us, everything great, and here is a picture full of puzzles, full of greatness, full of deep and beautiful questions, and likewise full of deep, majestic, and beautiful answers. It is a wonderful picture, and one is amazed that a human being of the nineteenth century was capable of painting it, for it really is painted as if a primitive Christian master had been its author. As grand as it is simple, as gripping as it is calm, as humble as it is ravishingly beautiful—such is the picture of the woman of Arles, whom one would like to approach without fluster, as a supplicant, with the question: "Tell me, have you suffered much?" One moment it is the portrait of woman as such, and then again it is the picture of life's cruel riddle in the shape of the woman who served as the painter's model, his model woman.

Everything in the picture is painted with the same solemn Catholicism, the same unswervingly faithful, earnest, and austere love, the sleeve as much as the headgear, the chair as much as the red-rimmed eyes, the hand as much as the features, and the mysterious, powerful stroke and flourish of the brush are altogether so leonine that one cannot help but feel, before something so titanic, defenseless. And yet it is still just a picture of a woman in everyday life, and precisely this mysterious quality is the grandeur that grips and shakes you. The background of the picture is like the inevitability of hard fate itself. Here a human being is pictured exactly as she lives, breathes, has her being as necessity long ago accustomed her to emotions she must quietly keep to herself, while she has perhaps halfway forgotten everything, everything she has had to endure, set on one side, and overcome. One wants to caress her cheeks, this long-suffering woman. The heart tells one to take off one's hat before the picture, stand there uncovered, as when one enters the sacred vault of a church. And isn't it strange, yet really not strange, how the painter who suffered so much (for he did) came to paint the long-suffering woman? She must have appealed to him immediately, boundlessly, and then he painted her. This being, cruelly treated by the world and by fate, who now has perhaps become cruel herself, was a sudden, immense experience for him, an adventure through the soul. Also I've heard people say that he painted her several times.

June 1912: Kunst und Künstler. SW 15.

Brentano

He no longer saw a future before him, and the past, however hard he tried to find some clarity in it, seemed a thing incomprehensible. The justifications crumbled away and desires seemed to vanish forever. Travels and wanderings, once his secret joy, had become strangely repugnant; he was scared to take a single step, and at every change of address he trembled, as if something monstrous confonted him. He was neither honorably homeless nor honestly and naturally at home anywhere in the world. He'd have liked so much to be a hurdy-gurdy man or a beggar or a cripple, then he'd have cause to ask people for sympathy or alms, but even more fervently he wished for death. He was not dead, yet dead he was, not beggarly poor, but such a beggar yet still he didn't beg, he still carried himself with elegance even now, like a tedious machine he still made his bows and spoke empty words, and was dismayed and horrified to be doing so. How tormenting his own life appeared to him, how false his soul, how dead his miserable body, how alien the world, how vacant the motions, things, and events that surrounded him. He'd have liked to drop into an abyss, to climb a glass mountain, be spread-eagled on a rack, with pleasure slowly burned as a heretic. Nature was like an exhibition of paintings, and through the galleries he walked with his eyes closed, feeling no temptation to open them, for with his eyes he had already seen through everything. It was as if he saw clean through people to their miserable entrails, as if he heard them thinking and knowing, only to see them commit errors and follies, stupidity, cowardice, and infidelity, and finally he felt he was himself the most fickle, lustful, and unfaithful of them all, of all things on earth, and he'd have liked to scream, call aloud for help, sink to his knees and weep aloud, sob for days and weeks. But he wasn't capable of it, he was empty, hard, and frosty, and at the hardness that filled him he shuddered. Where had the effusions gone, the enchantments he'd felt, where the love that winged him,

3

the goodness that glowed through him, the endless oceanic confidence he believed in, the God who flashed through him, the life he embraced, the ecstasies and glorifications that embraced him, the forests he wandered in, the green that refreshed his eyes, the sky into whose aspect he lost himself? He didn't know anymore than he knew what he should do and what must become of him. O, his person. To tear it away from the essence in him that was still good, that's what he'd have liked. To kill one half of the self, so that the other might not perish, so that the good in him might not be entirely lost. Everything was still beautiful to him and yet at the same time atrocious, still so dear and good and yet so ravaged, and everything was nocturnal, and deserted, and he was his own desert. Often, hearing a note of music, he thought he could die again back into his old, hot, sensitive fastnesses, into the mobile, rich, warm strength of yesteryear. It was like being skewered on the summit of an iceberg, terrible, terrible.—

Walking, he moved unsteadily, like someone in a fever, or drunk, and he had the feeling that the houses were going to collapse on top of him. The gardens, tended as they were, seemed to lie there sad and sprawling, he believed no longer in any pride, any honor, any pleasure, any true, genuine sorrow, or true and genuine joy. The solid, gorgeous fabric of the world now seemed to him a house of cards; a mere breath, one step, one light touch or movement, and it would collapse, a heap of slips of paper. How silly, and how atrocious.—

He didn't dare go the social rounds, in panicky fear that people could notice what a bad, what a desolate state he was in; to visit friends and talk things out—the mere thought of it pained him worst. Kleist was inaccessible, a sad, grandiose, Johnny-Go-Lightly, out of whom not a word could be got. Kleist was like a mole, a man buried alive. The others were horrors to him, so horribly confident, and the women? Brentano smiled. It was something between the smile of a child and that of a devil. And he made a dismissive, timid gesture. And then his many, many memories, how they mortified him, how they martyred him. The evenings brimming with melody, the blue and dewy mornings, the hot, crazy, steaming, wonderful noon hours, the winter, his most favorite season, the autumn—stop thinking about it. Everything must disperse, like yellow leaves. Nothing must stand, nothing have value, nothing, nothing must remain.

A girl of good family and with a beautiful and clear mind spoke to him as follows: "Brentano, tell me, don't you frighten yourself, living like this, having no higher values, no content to your life? Must it come to this, that a person one could love, respect, and admire, comes to deserve, almost, one's aversion? Can a person whose feelings are so many and so lovely be at the same time so unfeeling, must you always let yourself be carried away, scattering yourself and splitting up your faculties? Get a grip on yourself. You say that you love me? And that through me you'd become happy and true and sincere? Yet, O horror, Brentano, I can't believe what you say. You're a monster, you're a dear person, but a monster, you should detest yourself, and I know that you do so, I know that you detest yourself. That said, I won't waste another word on you. Please go away."

He leaves, and he returns, he pours out his heart to her, in her presence he feels something wonderful welling up in himself, he keeps telling her of his desolation and of his love, but she remains strong and firm and explains that she is his friend, but that's how things will stay, and that she can never be his wife, nor does she want to, nor may she be, and she implores him to stop hoping it could ever happen. He's in despair, but she cannot believe his despair is deep and genuine. She invites him one evening to a gathering of very many refined and respected people, to whom he might read a few of his beautiful poems, he does this and earns loud applause. Everybody is delighted by the harmonious sound and vivid exuberance of these poems.

One year passes, maybe two. He doesn't want to go on living, and so he decides to take, as it were, the life that is such a burden to him, and he goes to the place where he knows there is a deep cavern. Of course he shudders on arriving there, hesitant about going on in, but he reflects, with a kind of delight, that there's no more hope for him, that he has nothing, has no desire for anything now, and he steps through the great dark door and descends, step by step, deeper and deeper, feeling after the first steps taken that he's been on his feet for days and days, and finally he arrives below, at the very bottom, in the quiet, cool, deeply secret crypt. Here a lamp is burning, and Brentano knocks on a door. For a long, long time he has to wait there, until finally, after such a long time of waiting, of fearing, he is spoken to, and he receives the grim command to enter, and in he steps, with a timidity that reminds him of his childhood, and then he's standing before a man, and this man, whose face is covered with a mask, bids him abruptly to follow. "You wish to serve the Catholic Church? Come this way." That is what the dark figure says. And from then on, nothing is heard of Brentano.

1913: *Aufsätze. SW* 3.

Writing *Geschwister Tanner*

The thrilling brilliance of the capital's somber streets, the illuminations, the people, my brother. Me in my brother's apartment. I'll never forget that simple three-room apartment. A heaven it seemed to me, with stars, moon, and clouds. Wondrous romanticizing, sweet wistfulness! My brother at the theater deep into the night, painting the stage-set. At three or four in the morning he'd come home, and there I still sat, bewitched by all the thoughts, all the lovely images that had been passing through my head; it was as if I no longer needed any sleep, as if my sleep, delicious, fortifying, were writing and being awake, as if writing at my desk were my world, my pleasure, restoration, and repose. The dark-colored desk, so old-fangled, as if it were an ancient wizard. Whenever I drew out its finely worked little drawers, sentences, sayings, and maxims, so I imagined, came leaping out of them. The snow-white curtains, the singing gaslight, the longish somber room, the cat, and all the ocean calm of the long pensive nights. From time to time I'd visit the frisky girls in the girls' tavern, that was part of it all. Regarding the cat, it always sat on the written pages I'd set aside and blinked at me so strangely, so questioningly with its unfathomably yellow eyes. Its presence was like that of a bizarre, taciturn elf. Perhaps I have much to thank that amiable, quiet animal for. Who can tell? I seemed indeed, the further I advanced with the writing, to be sheltered and protected by some kindly being. A veil was weaving itself around me, large, tender, sensitive. Of course, the liqueur in the sideboard ought to be mentioned. I addressed it no more than I might and could. Everything around me had on me a refreshing and invigorating effect. Certain conditions, circumstances, orbits are just there, never to appear again perhaps, or again only when least anticipated. Aren't anticipations and suppositions unholy, pert, and insensitive? The poet must ramble, must audaciously lose himself, must always risk everything, everything, must hope, should do so, should only hope.— I remember that I began to write the book trifling hopelessly with words, with all sorts of thoughtless sketching and scribbling.— I never hoped to be able to compose something that was serious, beautiful, and good. A sounder train of thought, and, along with it, the courage to create, emerged only slowly, but thus all the more rich in secrets, out of the gulfs of self-forgetting and of reckless disbelief.— It was like the sunrise. Evening and morning, past and future time and the exciting present lay as if at my feet, a terrain right there in front of me came to life and I thought that in my hands I could hold human activity, all human life, seeing it as vividly as I did. One image succeeded another and ideas played with each other like happy, graceful, well-behaved children. I clung delighted to the frolicking main idea, and as long as I went on busily writing, everything connected.

1914: Kleine Dichtungen. SW 4.

The Back Alley

Probably few people think well of the back alley, but I love it for its quaintness. At least this much is fairly certain: descriptions and accounts of avenues and boulevards do not shake my conviction, my pleasing belief, that in its own way the back alley is beautiful. Of all the streets in this city it has most tenaciously kept, so I think, the character and the stamp of tradition, and if I say that it could almost be a street in Jerusalem, with Jesus Christ, the savior and liberator of the world, riding modestly into it, that is because I'm thinking of certain of Rembrandt's touchingly beautiful representations of the biblical story. Indeed, with its passages and vaults, their half-bright, half-dark penury, the back alley recalls some drawings by the great master aforesaid, who wondrously shaped humble and inconsequential things.

Didn't I recently glance into a bewitchingly lovely little room off the back alley, an old, adorable, actually quite large and spacious room, nice, most adorable, cheerful, friendly, and painted green, and didn't the tailor's wife who lived there for twenty years tell me of her husband's sudden death? I really think I did. And I can say that at any time at all I could choose to occupy such a clean, warm little room as a quiet and respectable lodger.

Haven't I also, even at any time of the day and any season of the year, seen in the back alley, where the Salvation Army, among other institutions, has its place of assembly, something attractive, something worth attending to? I'm convinced that there is, for day after day I hurry along it, my head full of useable and unuseable ideas, and on every occasion, as I hasten onward, I think to cast an attentive eye on the shoemaker's workshops there, on the droll junk shops displaying horror novels like *The Vampire* or *The Countess with the Lion* or *The Secret of Paris*, on apothecary shops, druggists, greengrocers and general groceries, businesses for leather and for butter, butchers and bakers. I speak perhaps of matters entirely commonplace and completely uninteresting when I report that recently three philosophizing workmen, whose simple and firm features and bearing pleased me very well, were standing in front of the rosily picturesque carnal splendors of a butcher shop, in the brilliance of the window's evening illumination, and with astonishment assessing the prices. I saw them with genuinely profound acumen studying the many varieties of meat displayed, such as veal and beef roast, stewing beef, cutlets, kidneys, brain, and liver, and I heard one of the men—they seemed unable to tear themselves away from the splendors—say most earnestly and slowly: "Tongue one franc forty." I was most thrilled to hear the dictum, for I must candidly say that I'm one of those who love the folk tone. To me and perhaps a few others the simple, honest, unadorned folk-saying means much more than anything that might be heard in the domains of distinguished and refined people. In the folk voice there is indeed something significant, like a deep call homeward.

Next I have to do with an apparently doughty warrior, insofar as I met recently in the back alley a young man, slim, very good-looking, walking on crutches, whom I supposed to be, on account of his lameness and of the unusually earnest look he gave me, an officer, one that had been in the war. The handsome young man's austere and earnest expression was something of a reminder to be earnest and high-minded in critical times. The figure he cut was most distinguished and noble. I believed I could at once understand the beautiful language of his eyes, but the young man wasn't perhaps what I supposed, and my speedy assumption might rest on an error. Even then, I'd received a beautiful and good impression, and with that I declared myself contented.

Might now two poor little back-alley boys be too trivial to warrant the gentle reader's attention? I hardly think so, for I consider everyone reading this a friendly, warm-hearted person. Later I'll speak of a lady who is shopping for Christmas in a bookshop. I'll employ poetic license to bring the lady into a certain relation with the boys. Of the two little lads it must be said that they seemed like brothers, that they were busy playing, when at noon I was hurrying along the alley, and that they rolled around like two balls almost, that they were wearing thick winter clothes and thereby resembled, as I just said, round things rolling on the alley, that they were calling, or rather, shrieking to one another, in hoarse, overloud voices, all sorts of apparently most important remarks. When I saw them playing I told myself that life since time immemorial has only been a game and in future will evidently remain so, though a game, of course, that is rich in destinies and coincidences. One of the boys called to the other: "Stay there!" This call was peculiar, insofar as it revealed a high degree, even the highest possible degree, of the joy of life and of youth. "Kings and emperors," I told myself, "their crowns do not shine and shimmer so purely as these poor boys' pleasure at playing. How grand and rich children at play are. All other joys pale beside the joy of childhood." Out of their shrill and actually quite unpleasant and raucous voices there was squeezed a truly delightful tenderness between brothers and children. "How these two lads do love one another. Will they always do so? How will things go for them later?" I thought, and, while I was thinking, I noticed two significant things about the boys: Their wonderful and pure childhood happiness, and along with it their lamentable, pitiful back alley poverty, or, somewhat otherwise expressed, the golden, glittering crown, the lofty jewel, the sunny and wonderful essence of joy, and along with it, in the bare wintery alley, their jarring, poor, half-frozen voices.

When then in the late afternoon I saw the refined, distinguished, well-dressed lady making her Christmas purchase in the elegant and well-lit bookshop, the earth, earthly life, and the play of human society seemed to me puzzling and strange, though not in any bad and wicked sense, rather in a beautiful and good sense. The lovely woman, the pervasive good taste and atmosphere of learning, culture, and instructive diversion made me on impulse attentive to myself, to the two poor back-alley boys, to the approaching night of Christmas, and to the singular dream called the world, and I said to myself: "What gifts will the two boys receive at Christmas? Will there be someone to give them something to enjoy? Will there be a Christmas Tree lit up in their little room? Will there be some-one to be a bit kind to them? Will there be someone to speak to them tenderly? And all the other children? Will all the other children have somebody who thinks of them, who brings them, and says to them, something nice?"

December 1916: *Der Bund. SW* 16.

The Story of the Prodigal Son

If a country squire hadn't had two sons who luckily differed from one another entirely, an instructive story could never have come into being, namely the story of the prodigal son, which tells that one of the two different sons was distinctly easygoing, whereas the other's conduct was egregiously sound.

Where the one seized the offensive, so to speak, early on, and marched off into the world, the other carefully stayed at home and persisted, as tenaciously as anyone possibly could, in a watchful, defensive position. Where the former, again, vagabonded about, so to speak, abroad, the latter seemingly loitered, so to speak, in a most respectable manner about the house.

Whereas the first was just up and away, the second clung to the home turf with astonishing constancy, discharging his daily obligations with unbelievable rigor. Whereas, again, the other found nothing better to do than flit and sail away, the other unfortunately proposed no more sensible plan than virtually to perish of practicality, steadiness, propriety, and usefulness.

When the son who escaped, the prodigal one, to whom the story owes its title, noticed bit by bit that his stocks were, indeed, at a rather, if not awfully, low ebb, he started off back home, which was doubtless quite sensible of him. The son who'd stayed at home would also have liked to start off back home for once, but the pleasure was denied him, quite simply, it can be supposed, because he'd never left it, but had stayed there, as we already know.

If it may be supposed that the runaway earnestly regretted having run away, then it may also be supposed or assumed that the one who stayed at home regretted his homeboundness more deeply than he'd anticipated. If the prodigal devoutly wished he'd never been prodigal, then the other, that's to say the one who'd never left, just as devoutly, or even more devoutly, wished that he hadn't stayed at home all the time, but rather had made good his escape and got himself lost, or that accordingly he might have very much liked to want to find his way home.

Since the prodigal son, after being long-believed lost, suddenly one evening put in a fresh appearance, a picture of destitution, in rags and tatters, it was as if the dead had more or less come back to life, whereupon for love all naturally made a wild rush at him.

The doughty one who'd stayed at home would have liked to be well and truly dead too and anon well and truly living again, so as to be able to have the experience of everyone for love naturally making a wild rush at him.

Joy at the unexpected reunion and delight at such a lovely and earnest event flashed and glowed bright and high like a conflagration all around the house, whose inhabitants, servants, and maids almost felt raised up to heaven. The homecomer lay outstretched on the floor, from which his father, had he been strong enough, would have lifted him. The old man wept so copiously and was so feeble that he had to be supported. Tears of bliss. In all the eyes there was a glint, in all the voices a tremor. Engulfed in such multifarious sympathy, in such sincerely loving understanding and forgiveness, the fallible son must have seemed almost a saint. Guilt only entitles the guilty, at such a lovely moment, to be lovable. Everyone was talking, smiling, making gestures in all directions, so much so that all the eyes to be seen were happy and at the same time moist, all the words were kind and at the same time grave. The felicitous event left not a cranny unillumined, for into the hindmost recess small and faint resplendences from the general splendor, little lights from the great light, pressed their way.

Any doubts cannot but be due to the fact that a certain other person would also have liked to be the object of such great joy: he who had never in his life got into debt would also very much like to have got for once some debts. He who always wore a decent overcoat would also very much like for once in a while to be seen in torn and ragged clothes. Very probably he'd have liked extremely well to lie full length, in pity-arousing rags, on the floor from which his father would have wanted to lift him. He who had never made a mistake would perhaps also very much like to have been a sinner. To be a prodigal son, under such favorable circumstances, was a real pleasure, but to him the pleasure was forever denied.

In the midst of gratification and contentment should we not hope that nobody but he remained disgruntled and cross? Yes, indeed. In the midst of communal happiness and amity, should we not hope that nobody but he remained chagrined and ill-disposed? Yes, indeed.

What became of the other persons I don't know. Very probably they died in peace. The odd and dissatisfied one, though, is still living. Recently he visited me, in fact. He introduced himself, mumbling and grumbling, as a man distressed to be connected with the story of the prodigal son, which he can only, with the utmost emphasis, wish had never been written. To the question I put him, as to how this might be understood, he replied that it was he who had stayed at home.

I wasn't for a moment startled at the uneasiness of this extraordinary oddball. His peevishness I entirely understood. That the story of the prodigal son, in which he clearly played a hardly commendable role, should be a pleasant and edifying one, I consider impossible. Indeed, I was thoroughly persuaded that the opposite was the case.

November 1917:
Neue Zürcher Zeitung. SW 16.

The Cave Man

Having been kindly invited to do so, we will say something about the mysterious cave man who emerged many thousands of years ago in Europe and elsewhere.

To the life he lived, esteemed listeners, there cannot possibly have been much variety; quite the reverse, that life was beyond question monotonous in the extreme.

Virtually no manuscript traditions, records, documents and suchlike have come down to us from the freezing wet, foggy grey, most probably vague and boggy ice and stone ages. Nevertheless, we know that the cave man inhabited fortuitous natural, and presumably very uncomfortable, refuges or caves.

In those days there would hardly have existed dwellings with five or six rooms, with appurtenances such as running water, an attic, a cellar, a balcony, maid's room, bathroom, central heating, and so on.

As everybody knows, architecture only began with the lake-dwellers, who constructed, though not in stone, perfectly decent houses. Although these lake-dwellers may well have been comparatively ignorant, rather than cultivated, they were doubtless intrinsically nice, sensible people.

As regards progress and civilization, from Charlemagne onward things were evidently looking up, insofar as there was such a thing, for instance, as the Christian religion. That man, extremely intelligent as he was, and hence egregious, introduced compulsory education, which had favorable consequences. Today we have a flowering of general conscription, without question an achievement of the first rank. But what cultural basis worth mentioning was ever achieved by the cave man?

I venture the opinion that he had absolutely no such ground on which to stand.

As regards his appearance, one can justifiably suppose that he had neither a hat on his head nor a garment on his body, nor boots nor shoes to wear on legs and feet. The accoutrement of an elegant suit, unthinkable. If he had no animal skin with which to cover himself, he walked around jay-naked, which may have looked rather to his disadvantage. Supposedly he was distinguished by hollow cheeks, horribly huge eyes, an unbelievably snub nose, unhelpful lips, coarse hands, and a conspicuous thinness. A fuzzy thick covering of hair protected him from wet and cold, otherwise he'd have perished most miserably.

Not for one moment need we doubt that his was a sad plight, that his condition was of the poorest. He was deprived of everything but privation. Accordingly he lacked just about everything anybody can. It should disconcert us to picture sympathetically a being so savage and so resourceless.

With soap, ladies and gentlemen, he would probably have longed to wash himself. That useful substance had, unfortunately, not by a long chalk ever penetrated his domestic domain.

About him there was not a single trace of the watch, the walking stick, the shirt, glove, or collar, and the merest thought of such conveniences as thread, scissors, needles, shoestrings, buttons, and suspenders, never entered his head, where anyway it could hardly have looked otherwise than indescribably dark, indeed most forlorn.

With the question whether it was preferable to lie at night in a bed or on the hard ground he would scarcely have needed to concern himself, because English and other beds, the bed frame, the mattress, the sheet, and the wool blanket were quite unknown to him.

Did he, first thing in the morning, painstakingly comb his hair? Otiose effort! Combs, with which rough and tousled hair can be set in order, did not exist in those days. Equally nonexistent were the water jug, the wash basin, and the towel.

Who would hasten willingly to change places with a person incapable of polishing, to the point desired, his teeth with a brush? For the poor lamentable cave man methodical care of the body was not possible.

Just as rough and hard as his couch was his diet. It is doubtful whether he knew how to light a fire. The state of his cuisine was hideous. Mostly he took his food cold. On that score, nobody will envy him much.

Any sort of entertainment was utterly remote. He had few or no pastimes. Pleasures, such as coffee to drink, beer, or tea, or feasts of chocolate, he dispensed with entirely. Card games and bowling were virtually unknown to him. Going for walks would not have been the thing to do. Theaters, concerts, exhibitions of paintings he attended seldom, or rather, not at all. Probably he never made formal calls. Newspapers and magazines did not exist. It is no exaggeration to say that he read little. Travel, sailing, and such activities were in those days all too complicated and hazardous, regret the fact as we may. It was not vouchsafed to him to attend instructive lectures. No church was there, fragrant with incense to stimulate reverential feelings, for him to enter; such comfort he never did enjoy. If we fathom our conception that in those days schooling, education, or suchlike brightening institutions were not in the realm of possibility, then a profound horror, mixed with sadness and pity, grips us, envelops us, and impulsively we exclaim: "How empty, how miserable! Ah, you poor fellow!"

Did he speak a language of some sort? Was he dreaming, or awake? Was he insane, or did he reason? Was there any such thing as reason in those days? Wasn't everything still erratic, gluey, welling up, stuck? Were there times when he smiled or wept? Was he, in some way or other, animated? Did he to some extent distinguish pleasure from pain, order from disorder, blessing from curse? Had he acquired a sense of good and evil, right and wrong, dutiful conduct and suchlike? Did any love for humankind ever dawn on him? Such difficult questions we will shelve, that's to say, leave unanswered for the time being.

Since he had almost no utensils, he practiced no profession, whence for him there were neither weekdays nor Sundays. Not a glimpse of cheerful, enjoyable handiwork came his way. Without the slightest difficulty we can readily understand that the beautiful turn of speech, "When he came home tired from work . . . " had no place in the world of the cave man, for he had no inkling at all of regular activity. His chief occupation consisted in worrying day after day how to preserve his bare existence. Apart from that, hunting for the stark necessities of life must have been (with more than sufficient reason) his everyday business. Hunger, thirst, and privation, fear and exhaustion, waiting and trembling in an unspeakable wasteland—such was his loathsome fate. His joyless and uneventful existence, menaced by constant mortal perils, cheek by jowl with monstrous animals, cannot possibly have been anything but frightful. Esteemed listeners, you, and this speaker, would gratefully reject an existence even remotely like this, that's for sure; for you and I, who are, God be thanked, members, so to speak, of a human society that has climbed the highest peak of culture, or at least appears to have done so, would not be able to endure such a naked, penurious life for twenty-four hours, let alone for months and years on end.

A firm conviction establishes itself: that the level he lived at was beyond description, inferior, and a person who passes his time not without sympathy but is capable of looking back from an elevated point of view, capable thus of an inner life, who thinks not only of his own existence but now and then of existences alien to him, who still dwells in mind somewhat on more remarkable matters than humdrum mechanical routines, who is aggrieved, too, when he finds himself absorbed without residue into superficial daily goings-on, for whom a reminder of the human he ultimately is does no offence to the surface glitter of his consciousness—such a person will have no choice but to admit that only a wonderful courage, a courage high above the scope of any flat imagining, enabled earlier man to overcome the ghastliness of everything around him. When we recognize the sheer labor of it, when we picture this heroic struggle, our pride, so puffed up with trinkets and with mannered mediocrity, must shrink for shame.

We are workers, Christians. But what was he? All around him were things I cannot speak of, things to him incomprehensible. For a variety of pleasures we are perhaps not nearly thankful enough, because our well-being and the blessings of our conventions have become mechanical.

All of us, couldn't we be a little readier to help and to please each other?

Untiringly, we imagine, he will have studied ways to refine and to ennoble his situation; for every feeling and thinking person it must remain a matter of amazement that he, ringed by conditions of extreme distress and by throngs of difficulties, relying entirely on his powers of resistance and on a spark of genius—a parting gift to lighten his journey—was not wiped out, but patiently propagated himself. Where would we be if he had wavered, failed, and if his so heavily taxed patience had ever been exhausted? Would you, dear and honored fellow-citizens, be able to eat, sleep, think, speak, walk, work, converse, climb mountains, read books, press loved ones to the heart, briefly, be alive, if he had not remained erect in the midst of inconceivable ordeals? Would we exist at all if that fellow had not proved himself firm-willed, steadfast, and persevering? I have already indicated elsewhere that the word "thank" derives from "think," so that thanklessness is simply thoughtlessness. Here I repeat unhesitatingly the reference, for it touches on concerns of fundamental importance, such as, I might say, the preservation of the state. By an overwhelming majority of people some phenomena of extreme gravity are barely noticed, because they are self-evident.

Firmly believing that for all of us nothing is so beautiful and so grand as that which we do, for a moment, comprehend, just so long as it suits us, I will break off here and take my leave.

May 1918: *Neue Zürcher Zeitung. SW* 16.

Dreaming

I imagine China to be a country of love and peace, where the laws are as soft as the breeze that wafts across regions where gracious behavior is everything. Cities and countrysides are like songs being sung by poets, and heaven is closer to earth than anywhere else. Why do I picture it so?

If there are good people anywhere, then they are living in China, which is a sort of empire of the center. Nobody there is so foolish as to believe himself better than his fellow beings. I think of the Chinese as people polite and happy in equal measure, as friendly as they are helpful. There, modesty is the crowning glory of sentiment. Everyone keeps the well-being of everyone else in view.

In China, nobody is arrogant. To no person does it occur that he alone deserves consideration, while others should be so kind as to put up with its absence. Shouldn't every mature human being be fully desirous to see his neighbor enjoying prosperity, seeing to his own only if that is so?

In those regions little children drink in the idea of brotherliness with their mother's milk, the premise of which is that the parents are affectionate and serious people. On streets and in the plazas, in forest and field, one person looks upon another with sympathy, as if saying: "I'm at your disposal. I mean to live only for your good."

In China, nobody is imprudent, for people are trustful and receptive to friendship. Doesn't everyone who behaves with heart go irresistibly to heaven? Elsewhere there is so much treachery and worry in equal measure, there are equally many attacks of weakness and of rudeness, there is as much fear as there is mockery, misery, and pitilessness. What makes a country great is nothing but the good condition of all its members.

A Chinese woman looks like a flowering plant. To think of China in springtime makes one happy. The language is like a delicious drink; to speak it is bliss, the words are sweet as kisses.

On the rivers swim barques abounding with pleasures and with music.

Bridges span the delicate waters. On the shores grow trees like veils. Delectable slopes are densely covered with houses. Everything sensuous is neighbor to everything good. The morning has an enchanting glow, and in the evening everyone is drunk with tenderness and contentment.

Everything is concerted, work with entertainment, serious things with pleasurable things. Over pathways soft as carpets beautiful young maidens go riding on zebras or gazelles and cannot help smiling all the time. In a blue haze, among greenish shrubs, lie adorable villages with reddish-brown roofs.

Everyone who is healthy goes to work. The old people are honored, the sick lovingly cared for. China is teeming with people, but nobody vexes anyone; the Chinese are versed in everything social as the most important thing in existence.

On the mountains stand temples which are consecrated to the gods. Innumerable lamps shimmer at night. Behind the house there is a garden where birds twitter in the moonlight or in the sunshine.

The human traffic is like an ocean. All people have only good intentions. Evils and sorrows have long been overcome.

1920: *Schweizerland. SW* 16.

Hercules

His birth was brilliant. If I'm not mistaken he was the outcome of an illicit relationship. He was the son of a princess and of divine descent. Zeus, his father, sneaked into bed one night with Amphytrion's wife, to enjoy himself, and in so doing he succeeded. The boy gave early proofs of remarkable strength. Probably he preferred sport and that sort of thing. We know nothing of his schooling. Perhaps he didn't even go to school. It seems to us that he must have assigned more value to physical than intellectual development. His education was probably rather patchy. But one thing is certain, and that is the gigantic work he did, for he piled labor on labor. Thus, for example, he thoroughly cleaned a stable. Nowadays, of course, that wouldn't cause much of a stir. Also with his typical energy he purged an extensive landscape of all sorts of useless riffraff, successfully fought a lion, and lamed a highway robber who'd been pestering travelers, treating them in a manner they disliked. When the athlete thought he'd done enough and, tired by his exertions, was longing for a doubtless well-earned rest, he happened upon a lady who tied him up extraordinarily. The celebrated fighter now carried water, knitted socks, shook out pillows, peeled potatoes. Ah, what a comedown! But why complain? He who conquered terrors and performed great deeds now took a fancy to washing dishes, he stayed decently at home and obeyed a delicate little woman. A brawler became gentle-hearted and well-mannered. Such things do happen. May worse not befall us!

May 1920: *Das Tage-Buch*. *SW* 16.

Odysseus

Odysseus was said to be really shrewd; some people even thought him sly. In any case he was a capable person. He earned distinction in the war by erecting a wooden horse, about which the enemy made jokes, thereby deriding, sad to say, their misfortune. With this trick Odysseus unquestionably did great service. When Hector fell and Troy went up in flames, the gentlemen could return home; they did so, probably, with broad grins, and that was fine because nobody doubts that something thoroughly pleasant always accompanies success. However, the homecoming didn't run as smoothly as they'd supposed. Agamemnon's reception was hardly what he'd expected, an affair of joyous gunshots and proclamations of applause. Against Odysseus adverse winds got up. For Poseidon had a bone to pick with him and drove him every which way round the clock. In the course of his wanderings he had, indeed, all sorts of interesting adventures, experiencing joys and sorrows such as nobody else has, wasted much time in dalliance, since he consorted often and energetically with women, which may have been as much to his detriment as to his advantage. He only just squeaked past the Sirens. He spent years in the vicinity of a lady who had the wicked habit of transforming men with apparently good reputations and solid ways of life into what is best not closely described. Finally he reached home, but heard about a crowd of suitors enjoying themselves in his own bailiwick and courting his wife. He chanced to pick up a newspaper and read in print about himself as somebody who probably lost his way wherever he was. He carefully remained disguised, until the moment came when he stood up to be recognized; at his appearance the suitors scattered in all directions, and then he could step across to his wife.

July 1920: *Das Tage-Buch*. SW 16.

Theseus

As Jakob Burckhardt teaches us, what mattered to the Renaissance Italians was culture, education too, as well as the cultivation of personality. After all they were, in part, still people of ancient times. How did it look in brightly shining Hellas? Medea ate her children. What did Theseus do? Furnished with strength, abilities, and joie de vivre, he undertook journeyings that brought him into all parts of the world as it then was. Of course, the Cape of Good Hope didn't exist yet. Was it for him a question of learning foreign languages? We doubt it; rather we believe he traveled because he wanted to have experiences, for plainly he was not someone to remain sedentary for long. That's how I construe it, though I grant anyone the right to a different opinion. So off he went and had countless romances, until he came to a kind of labyrinth, into which he absolutely had to go, though he was advised against it. Armed with nothing but his courage and his really fabulous self-confidence, he went on in. Well, a girlfriend named Ariadne gave him a string to take along on the one-and-only journey, and he in no wise rejected it, because he knew he'd be able to use it. How long it took him to reach the center we do not know; once there, in any case, he had to fight with an ox, or a mammoth, and he did so with every success. After this, he took care to get away, and saw daylight again, which presumably pleased him. When he came home to his own people, lots of silly things happened. Phaedra had fallen in love with Hippolytus, who was extremely handsome, and this occasioned a tragedy, which hit him hard. He was said to be, all in all, a skirt-chaser, and accordingly he was, alas, rather frivolous. The way he neglected his family gives pause for thought. Nonetheless, he promised to mend his ways. Wasn't his son a more serious person than he was?

September 1920: *Das Tage-Buch. SW* 16.

Olga's Story

Olga was telling her story: I came from a petit bourgeois family; that may be why I later shied away from everything petty. We don't ever love our surroundings as much as what's different and strange.

My parents love me, I love them too. In school I had the hardest time sitting still; but the teachers treated me kindly, I flirted with them.

One of my brothers was a store-clerk. Me, I wrote to a bookseller: "I want to be where there are lots of books. Will you accept me?"

He replied: "Come along, I'll try you out." So I learned the book trade, though only superficially. I leafed through all sorts of books, just as I pleased; gradually I became quite literary. What's more, the owner was always satisfied with me.

Some people said I was uncouth. Certainly I behaved more according to my moods than to rules of reason, and I was always somewhat excited. If they saw something of a wild animal in me, perhaps they judged me rightly. A working woman really didn't have to watch out for her deportment.

Sometimes I just couldn't be bothered about anything. But I think it's wrong to be alive and not set value on life. I was always searching for something.

Once a famous actress came to the city theater. I waited for her and gave her a bunch of roses. She took them, thanked me, gave me a deep look, asked me something, but then suddenly she hadn't the time, said goodbye, and she'd vanished.

That evening I was happy, I looked in the mirror and wished I had a lover.

Isn't there something magnetic about our thoughts? The next day I had him. Who was he? Well, my gallant. Was he very gallant? No, not in the least, and I was glad that he wasn't. I don't like to have people serve me. I'd rather do the leaping and serve myself.

So now I had a friend, I thought it heaven, my dear one was all I could ask for.

He was poor, but like a genius; he studied at college and had lunch and dinner with well-off people. They invited him because he was clever, so frank, and his talk was a blazing fire.

Often as he was in society, he loved solitude, for he wrote poems, and everything he wrote, he gave it to me to read, and it was all about love, nothing else, and of course about love for me. Wasn't it marvelous? Could flowers smell sweeter?

It hardly occurred to us to kiss. A glance, a pressure of the hand, that was enough. We had such a good opinion of ourselves that we didn't know how we'd come to believe in one another. The sun shone only for us, for us the moon shed its beams.

Once he gave a lecture, and when he was applauded and publicly praised, I thought him the best man in the world and right there and then I fainted.

Certainly he was a good person, I have no more doubts about it now than I had then; but a woman snatched him away from under my very nose, sort of; I could only watch him walk away. She found him charming, and soon he became her husband.

One day they visited me, for he'd told her about me. He wanted her to meet me, so we'd be friends.

When they came to me I was aghast and shouted: "Do you want to torment me?"

She answered gently: "Not at all, dear child, I'll do anything to make you happy. We've come to ask if you'll come to live with us."

"That's impossible," I said, but, right after, I had another idea, and I added: "Yes, all right."

Then she kissed me, I kissed her, too. I came to love her, and because I felt superior to her, I was able to behave decently. By yielding I was lifted up.

What's more, I thought her so kind that it wasn't difficult for me to be nice to her. We suited one another, and consequently I believed I'd won my game to some extent. She asked me to be her companion; I declared I was her maid and said, besides, all sorts of thoughtless things.

Now I was living with them, and it was like a dream. I did everything in a sort of sleep, like someone who feels and understands nothing, yet does distinctly feel and understand. This made me more cheerful than the others.

Now and then I'd glance at him, press his hand, but I said nothing, and she got more and more serious.

One day she said I'd better leave them. She was not satisfied, she was unhappy; actually it was me who should have been so. Now things had changed.

So I went away, back to office-work, came into contact with people, had women friends, who really didn't concern me closely.

Frequently life seemed to me like a cramped little house on the edge of everything, because it was so insignificant; yet I loved it and tried to be warm with everyone.

Among the people I'd come to know there was an earnest, quiet person, half shut, half open and cheerful, very intelligent, but at the same time childlike and inclined to believe there to be, somewhere, something beautiful, except that he was unable to see it, or was too inept to haul it aboard.

He read a lot, gave me books, too. When they were too difficult for me, I set them aside, since I didn't want to strain my wits unnecessarily.

Yet that's just what he did, very much so, and at times he had a suffering look. He squandered his knowledge on me and others, in conversation; it was a pity, I told myself, that he didn't turn it to better account.

He had no thought of being famous; human beings were his concern. While he talked and I interposed remarks, it seemed to me that he was surprised at himself for having anything to do with me. But then of course he liked me, and that was something else.

I think he never knew what he was all about, regarding himself and others. Perhaps his own character disturbed him. Several times he confessed to me that he was in need of peace and quiet, but I thought what he needed was diversion, though I do realize that some people shun diversion, because it blurs the line they've drawn between day and night and tarnishes a tone that they can't live without.

To some people he seemed timid, but he wasn't so, he was just weary, weary because he hadn't met with deeper people. Ordinary life seemed to him a puppet show.

Possibly he'd have found what he longed for if he'd just gone out and grabbed it; but for making a decision one way or the other he was, in a way, almost too wise.

Soon I found myself in circumstances so new that I saw no more of him, and this amazed me, though again I looked on it as being quite natural.

A distinguished gentleman took a liking to me; I went for it, played the lady, as if I'd been one all along.

Horses and automobiles were at my disposition; in salons I was at the forefront. I took no joy in it, only pride, my willfulness gratified.

I forgot everything. The things one forgets, when one no longer knows oneself! The more I was concerned with etiquette, the less steady I was inside myself. But it all fell apart; came the day when I had nothing.

As soon as I was working again, the joy came back. A plain person wanted to tie the knot, his existence with mine; he spoke honestly and calmly; I loved him, and a sickness took him off.

I went to his grave; the sun was reddening the roofs and towers of the town and the crests of the trees.

It was impossible not to love the world, not to look cheerfully forward into life. That's how I am; what am I supposed to do about it?

July 1921: *Pro Helvetia. SW* 16.

Something about Goethe

He was still at odds with himself in many ways. Work lay unfinished, and a woman he was fond of didn't want him to leave. His obligations to her were such that her anger at him was almost justified; but he was also angry at himself, for owing so much to himself. Perhaps he alone, nobody else, understood. At bottom it was a feeling of life's richness that enabled him to risk quitting for a while his immediate concerns. He took the risk because he knew he simply had to.

The very first days of travel—and already he was opening up; he felt stronger inside, his ability to think becoming lighter, richer, soaring more rapidly over everything. A blue sky amiably accompanied him; as on he sped, agile clouds, driven by a decent wind, floated before him and flew in pursuit of him, for he, too, was in a hurry, though his conduct, in the rush for experience, was dignified.

By his absence, if not losing valuable patronage, still he might be diminishing it; but did this allow him therefore to flinch, to shun activities that would lift him up as a human being, enable him to swing into an orbit of discernment whence he might better see through events, whether pressing or gratuitous, and survey them? No, he must no longer hesitate. Didn't the goddess of fate herself point the way? The shining opportunity, did she not show him it? He saw, yes, how golden it was, and shimmering; with his inward eye he saw it, and the soul helped. When he returned, he'd make good everything he'd neglected. Surely unquestioning confidence was the basis of any capable action.

For the time being he now let himself go, even if it looked almost like a weakening of character. Firmness and tenacity of will must not lapse into rigidity. To stroll around now and then might mean having later to get all the more busy. He was enthralled to have found the strength that brings serenity, to have overcome ambition, or at least to have set it aside, ambition which lessens the pleasures of being human and inserts a timidity into every thought of it. Honors and esteem—by all means let others enjoy them.

Floated by the feeling that a modest position would be, if need be, quite enough, that there was no need at all to be first in line, he gave his attention to every breathing, living being, and in the best of ways diverted as well as developed himself. Already he could see ahead, into work that would come, happy creation, a continuation of what he'd begun and the start of something new.

With travelers he was communicative, losing confidence hardly for a moment. Unsure of ourselves our tendency is to say nothing. The words with which we treat our fellow-men are an unfailing sign of good feeling, a healthy heart. If his genius had brought him successes, now he was more and more glad to get along without recognition, to be able to move as a person unknown among unknown persons. Alert as he was to every circumstance, impression, influence, discriminating any least mark of self-love, his emergence as something like a great man had begun almost to numb him; it was as if he had been feeling weary of his good fortune, his enterprise.

Spirited, loving humanity enough to hold even himself under reproach, he placed the exhilarating majesty of life, in nature the eternal, above everything puny and vain. Nobody alive could be exempted from the status of equality; this was a hard law, but also one that was conciliatory, uplifting, fortifying; with that at one's back, one could stride twice as easily through the contradictions. He saw land-workers working the land, craftsmen at their crafts. The variety of incongruent persuasions conferred something panoramic on life. More vividly than ever before, he understood how good things and bad were on a par, as driving forces, how each grew out of the other, how each determined the other reciprocally.

Something he had long missed, had long postponed, this going easy, soul at rest, being carefree, this gift from heaven, that knowledge of being free, which the huntsman feels, and the shepherd, the Olympian thing, which makes life a matter for love alone—now he possessed and enjoyed it. One day he reached Zürich, and he was entranced at the aspect of the gracious city. With joy he had himself rowed over the lake, found, in a hastily sketched little love poem, expressions of a happiness akin to rocking over the delicate blue billows. He was amazed at himself, liked himself that way, and thought that much, much, many good things so long desired had now, unnoticeably, as in a dream, come to fruition. He'd have liked to have a kitten to stroke along with him, or a puppy, or better still, a girl.

Bells rang from the city, evening came; he had himself brought ashore, walked up the slope to Bodmer, whom he already knew from hearsay. Then there was a heartfelt greeting, he saw that he was welcome. In the beautiful house, full of cosy nooks, a room was arranged for him, every comfort provided.

At night, while everyone else was asleep, Goethe walked out of the house into the moonlit garden, where moths were flitting about the bushes. Here like a young man he dreamed, looked up to the sky, to the celestial regions, to the glittering constellations, friendly planets, and thought in his joy, in his self-oblivion, of a poem, and of good people faraway who were perhaps at this moment thinking of him.

A week later he took the ferry up the lake and traveled over the St. Gotthard Pass, on into Italy.

August 1921: *Pro Helvetia. SW* 18.

The Robber

A pretty woman loved a robber. She was rich, gave parties. Of him it can be supposed that he lived in a hut.

She wore loafers as well as high-heel shoes, and she thought well of him because he was brave, and fair match for hundreds. What an interesting affair.

She had a cage full of lions and tigers and tubs full of snakes. What had he got? Countless sins on his conscience. But at least he wasn't dull. That decided it.

His overcoat was threadbare enough, it's true; but she went about with unbelievable chic.

They met partly in the mountains, partly at the railroad station. He consigned all his loot to her by bank draft.

Sometimes he'd visit her, and on such occasions he wore an impeccable suit. His behavior was always very polite.

He read Stendhal, she read Nietzsche. This is no place for explanations, even if requests come in for an entire year.

She never permitted intimacies. Their relations remained platonic, and rightly so, for otherwise he'd have lost his spirit of enterprise.

He was a Napoleon! And she? A Catherine the Great, perhaps? Not in the least.

She was the proprietor of a grocery who had three children, and our robber was a decent, reasonable young man, who was in love with the little woman, came into her little shop now and then, and chatted with her.

The tigers and lions, the polished bootees, dazzling parties, the impeccable suits, the hundreds he was a fair match for, the relationship full of sacrifices, the whistlings, signals, and shaggy hair, are figures of fantasy.

The person who hatched them now glances at the dial and thinks it is time to get up from his desk and go for a little walk.

October 1921: *Das Tage-Buch. SW* 18.

The One and Only

She to whom poems are addressed, who is significant, who writes no poems but is a poem significant to a poet—I know her. If one is fresh with her, she shows only glorious astonishment. I have sung her, but not yet to my satisfaction. She chased me off; at which I laughed, happily, as if she'd given me a night with her, such as leaves the poet cold, because he has long since been allowed by his imagination to see her limbs. After that, I'll never love again. She made of me a child who marvels at the earth, is subjected to beautiful instruction, and reveres God. Her shoes are not especially marvelous. But I do love the towel she toys with. I do not have permission to see her again, and yet, if it really should not be so, I'm happy. With her my behavior was shameful, for in her presence I trembled, and I tried to pretend I was superior to her and found this trembling, this love, foolish, and almost detested it. Yet, far from her, I caress her, play with her, caper like a lunatic, a silly boy. For four years I might be able to forget her, then everything would come over me anew. To know this, enchanting. Till then, I had no idea what power a girl has. All fidelity and whatever else is good in me comes to nothing against the vesture of the One and Only. I'm cheerful, as otherwise only in the early morning; but it is midnight. I write this out, as if giving it to nobody to read.

c. 1924/25, on the flyleaf of a copy of his poems (1919). April 1938: *Neue Zürcher Zeitung*, SW 17.

Finally she condescended

Finally she condescended. I gasp for breath already, I could swoon. The sophisticate, in her bright and beautiful attire. At any moment he might expect her in his home. He had summoned two servants, paid servants, you know, and they had cleaned everything. The furniture was aglow. On the table with its patched tapestry cloth stood a bouquet of flowers, or rather, to be precise, it did not stand directly on the table but in a container placed upon the table. The window with its windowpanes, well, take it from me, it made a shimmering display of light. The room positively swam in sunlight, and now, suspicious of herself and of him, too, she was coming up the staircase, which had been scoured till it was virgin pure. Her heart knew not what it felt, what it really wanted. With a splendor I'd willingly describe in copious detail, a wondrously opulent jewel, alluringly golden, was enthroned upon the sideboard, in an oblong case. The jewel was intended for the angel now quietly lowering her blond head at the door, though she wasn't thinking of anything. She was grumbling at herself for not sufficiently grumbling about him. So one may say that while knocking she was still playing her role as the fine indignant lady, the role she faithfully played throughout her life. A voice in the room called out, "Come in!" She went in, the room was empty. Not a leg to be seen, let alone a person. She liked the decor, she was amazed how clean it was. Every object seemed to welcome her with a benediction. I am outraged to be writing about this; I must make it clear, for instance, that the rascal, for such he seems to me, had no sooner called out "Come in!" than he hid himself in the wardrobe, to vex her ladyship. And vexed she was. "Well now, here's a to-do," she told herself in her childlike voice. There she stood. Then she saw the jewel. How on earth could she not have seen it before? Now she was grumbling to the jewel, which seemed to mean to make fun of her. "That rude fellow is hiding," she said. I almost said "whispered," but the word "whisper" is a bit rude, so I told myself to leave it out, if I didn't mind. The jewel reveled in its beauty. That sounds like something in a fairytale, but I'd better let it stand. Fairytales are still in demand, in life as in bookshops. People everywhere are seeking for experience, the real thing, wholesome, if possible. The best and most genuine people want simplicity to be restored. Well now, did he leap out? Ah! At this point I want so much to ferret out the right idea. No, he kept quiet. He let her stand there. Not a sound in the street, or in the room. This storybook silence is putting me to sleep. She listened. Inside the wardrobe, so did he. I'd also like to describe in copious detail how eager she was to embellish herself with the jewel. Really now, though, he could stop this pussyfooting around. A childish situation. It seemed interesting to him; she was vexed to be finding it tense. So she was the little child and he was the big one, or perhaps it would be just as well to think of him as the little child and of her as the big one. The difference is only slight. Then, having wasted a certain amount of her time, she went away. "I'll never come again," she vowed to herself. Did she keep her vow? We don't know. We do know that he leaped out of the wardrobe now and in raptures capered about the room. He was radiant.

September–December 1924. B 1.

The Fairytale Town

In this puppydog town I've become one of its lapdogs, wagging my tail. Poets here dine by invitation, with people of refinement. Housewives give them roses and the husbands don't complain. Till late in the night there are shimmering lights in the elegant patisseries. Cooling trees lift up their crowns while the whisper of music issues out of gardens all immured in leaves. The town—it's like a beautiful woman often and ardently courted, who concedes nothing, luckily, so she is always desired, loved, and courted. Oodles of schoolboys stroll in the arcades, and girls go adorned with feathers and funny whims. They aren't walking but dancing. In the morning, early, I'm fairly bowled along, upstairs, down-stairs. I recently drank all sorts of liqueurs in a hotel, which cost me a pretty penny, but a good thing should not be cheap, I think. In such surroundings it's no wonder I've come to be young. I play the fool for a while in bed, before I get out of it. There are little faces here to knock you down dead and awaken you smartly from a death full of delights. Spar-kling glasses, scarily pretty nosegays, glittering rings—and a whole heap of tasks undone. Sir, be sorry for me! Be envious! Here I learned to blow the flute, playfully. Benevolent in the vicinity rises a mountain, and up you go, evenings, climbing delicately looped paths, to gaze down upon the serenity and the splendor, wave a hand, extend an arm in greeting. This town of my love, of my many, many askings, this ribbony lapdog town is my domain. Never yet in my lifetime did I feel so safe and secure. Laughter often shakes me, it drips and trickles through my limbs. How wonderfully the woman grou-wouse and pou-wout. They want to be cour-wourted and la-waughed at, but that sounds coarse. Here I did discover my heart—and if I leave, which I can't bear to think of, it will bleed, I'll have to tear myself away by force. Still, I don't yet know this, I refuse to know about it. Not for a moment did I get bored here, and writing? I haven't written a line. Who'd ask a lapdog to write? What might become of me then? Is it a mishap to be happy? I won't tell the town's name, there's no need, as long as it's *schön*, as long as you like it.

February 1925:
National-Zeitung, Basel. *SW* 17.

The Blind Man

I pretended to be blind, groped for the orange peel, walked round chairs, threw the peel into the waste paper basket, with eyes closed drew my slippers on, walked to the balcony, everything went red in front of my eyes, as if I were watching a joyous wedding. Wind flew round my forehead and hair. I sensed the presence of God. "Helen," I stammered and at the same time felt like Oedipus being led by his daughters away from the scene of his misfortune into a green retreat, the lightnings of terror still flashing round him and yet already having a premonition of rebirth. Freedom's refraction was red, because freedom is green. When I stumbled back into the living room, a dark blue swam before my closed spirit, yet I don't know how I came to be comparing eyes with spirit. Anyway, I'm writing it down. Something higher than us is playing with us. I cannot evade the moods of gods and goddesses. Meanwhile I become conscious of growing older. People now just growing up will see me stooped, bent, tapping about. I undertook to settle at my desk. But when I opened my eyes I was standing in front of the clothes closet. I called: "Jocasta!" Another name occurred to me, too. I don't think blindness would make me unhappy, but I prefer not to say anything about that. For instance, I wouldn't see my lady friend again. Would that do me any harm? Could it grieve me? Absolutely not. My thoughts allow me at every moment to hold her lovely hand, and when to my ear I say, "Bring me her voice," I hear her whisper then, and if I'm without eyesight her mouth descends to my lips, and even if I cannot go to her, I'm lying in her arms.

April 1925: *Prager Presse.* SW 17.

And now he was playing, alas, the piano

And now he was playing, alas, the piano, making it sound like a deep and intimate promise, which isn't at all the way to start a novel. So Captain Rumbelow was present before her again, she sensed he was a danger as well as a solution. Who was this "she" but the decentest little average woman, and what could the homecomer be but the bravest of men-in-the-street, save that his moustache was no more than comparatively martial. Upon such persons music lays a consuming, intoxicating spell, at once they fancy themselves altogether at home in the château of a count and believe that masses of Manets hang on their papered walls. For a long time the poorest of husbands hadn't the faintest idea. Finally his eyes were opened and on page 112, to go so far as to seem most oddly exact, his face was distorted into a caricature, he uttered a dutiful groan; a suppressed cry, just the one the author ordered, wrenched itself from his soul. Rumbelow delivered a fervent speech on women's rights. Reading my way unflinchingly through numberless unwarrantable line-breaks, I skipped two hundred pages without a twinge of conscience, kept all the time some chocolate at hand, so as not to lose heart, and on a lovely green meadow arrived at the manly decision to set the book aside, considering it read, still noticing how the Rumbelow-loving associate of circles declaredly bourgeois did return to her domestic senses and to the child, and how Countess Cirke, but now I'm speaking of a manuscript whose author, allegedly seen at one time in the Niederdorf and then for years hidden from our sight, stood agitatedly at a window of her dainty little palace and was looking down into a garden swathed in a lamentation of nightingales, when the bell to the garden door chimed. The visitor's name was Spatz, an Indian brown his countenance, but "countenance"? It has too fine a sound for such a face as his. O so wonderfully tired he was. One can be incredibly young and incredibly despondent, thus was Spatz, who now abruptly said to the owner of the white villa: "So what did you do with the bouquet?" "What bouquet? Spatz, dear, I don't know of any flowers on your account, because you aren't somebody I know. But I like you, so I invite you to supper, I have a very nice big cat, who will also dine at our table." How quietly they now strode through a series of chambers into the corner room, where the windows were open. Not a breath of wind in the park outside, both of them felt hot as well as cold. Once the maidservant had brought their dishes and they were seated and eating, a high trembling voice sang out below: "Why must I pine away?" The mistress of the castle and the feast told her guest to pay not the slightest attention to sentimentalities, even if they themselves might be making gracious remarks, and she poured him a glass of the Macon, the carmine of which decorated the table, and daintily and spitefully she smiled: "An idiot begging me to release him from my power," she breezily added, and "I have charge of a number of freaks, which became drakes the moment they saw me, that's to say, came anywhere near me. What do you think of me?" Spatz said: "You are beauty and innocence in person." "Where are you from?" she asked, but she made no further allusion to his answer. "From wanderings on which I gathered chagrins and satisfactions, which is why I spoke of a bouquet, imagining I knew you, that I'd loved you and given you a bunch of the joys of life and of its sorrows." Here she let fall to the floor a tiny notebook. Spatz made no move. She picked it up by herself and a grumpy look came over her face. "Why are you not gallant?" her look asked him, and his replied: "Because otherwise you'd soon have enough of me." She smiled again, but this time it was a beautiful smile, and then like a goddess she subsided on the sofa, and let him kiss her? What? So soon? Of a practiced Cirze that's not to be believed, and it's not the case, either. No, all she did was let him look at her. Authors like me reflect for months, even years, before we allow a little kiss. And so she reclined there, and when she moved a bit the sofa pinged, charmingly it pinged beneath her charming weight. "Why aren't you crying? You should have done so long ago. The bard you just heard in the garden cries all night for me. Out of his tears I've had a ball-dress made, a sumptuous thing to wear." Spatz replied: "I still don't quite understand you. Once I worked in a trade. That made me rather seriously reasonable. I'm not so easily captivated, but you do make me feel, no doubt about it, rapt away." Then without a word of farewell to his hostess he went into the garden, lay down under the spreading branches of a fir tree, and sank into a deep sleep, in which he dreamed he was under an obligation to write a book and didn't know how to start it. When he woke up it was night, a voice was calling to him, it was hers, and on the instant another voice, and a third, and a fourth. When he'd listened enough and felt at peace, he went into the house and said to his mistress: "A long stay in literary circles has had a strong aesthetic effect on me. The same happens and has happened to lots of people. An excess of understanding can make it so one understands nothing." "That's not so bad," she observed, and we are of the same opinion. It's simply that people like Spatz think too much about themselves. But if they didn't do that, they wouldn't be called intellectuals, and Kirce resolved to shape him. "But haven't I seen you somewhere before?" he wanted to begin his investigations again. "Forget it, just think of me. Look at me! How unfriendly your eyes still are. They should be glinting." A chandelier, not a mere lamp, burned in the room, the interior of which we should now attend to. The walls were painted with forests, in which things were happening. "You can be my poet and take note of the stories I tell you." He nodded. Over the precipice into the abyss a loving couple fell, he wildly resolute, she desperately resisting. I saw the picture on canvas at the market one day in a little village where, from the houses, smoke was rising, because everyone was cooking at the time. O little novel, apparently subtle, ever strange, I will thus conclude you.

May–July 1925. B 1.

An Essay on Lion Taming

During this performance several people walked out. "We are frightened," they said, as if they considered themselves too precious even to survive a little fright. Yet fear, as such, is so interesting. I was afraid primarily for the tamer—others feared for him, too. I was telling myself: "After all, he could be a very pleasant fellow, and his profession is a difficult one." Well now, perhaps this profession looks more difficult than it is; it entails certain tricks, and it is based on a system. The lions were somnolent, sullen, you could see this at once; they take regular meals. During their prolonged deprivation of movement, those lions, so I conceive, get somehow de-lioned. At the same time they are dangerous. But while the lion tamer is in action, one sees a number of lions, which of course explains something, namely that it is harder to train a single lion than a company of them. Among Mormons, for instance, marriages provided for the husband a comfortable situation; they were prohibited on account of the comfort's being wicked and soporific. Mightn't there also be in military drills, to the clear eye, a similar sort of somnolence? This collective compliance. Of course I do not dispute the military's usefulness. Here I'm only making comparisons. The soldiers know that they'll be punished if they don't conform. The lions know it, too. The lions, if they so wished, could easily tear their dominator to pieces, just as mutinous soldiers, if they so wished, could with the greatest ease overpower their superiors, as Mormon wives, if they cared to, could incapacitate their master.

I permit myself to confess the following: I only glanced fleetingly at the actual person of the tamer, because I was afraid of doing him some harm. For, if I look at someone, I might be taking away his thoughts, his powers, I irritate him, cause him, as it were, to "dream." So I will be understood when I explain that consciously, that's to say, fearing for the tamer, I had looked at those points or surfaces which he commanded the lions to occupy. About strange influences we still know very little. For every emergency the lion tamer is equipped with an iron stick. Didn't Pippin the Small once fight a lion successfully? He contrived the fight so as to force people who ridiculed him to respect him, and that's precisely what he did. Taming is usually started early, when the subjects are very young, and of course this greatly simplifies the task. The boredom that lions experience in their cage is itself already a sort of training, taming, stultifying. The monotony to which the lions are doomed serves the tamer just as an active and capable assistant might. Inactivity, as everyone knows, leads to luxurious and soft living. The way they bobbed and bowed around him, as if they executed his wishes only with reluctance, was to me like music. Lions roar with glorious precision. One can call it precision. It's almost a shame, considering the leonine temperament. On the other hand, such beasts only lurk in wildernesses to pounce on living creatures and satisfy their tempestuous hunger. Here, since they are trained, the helpings they receive are none too large, but the diet is healthy, clean, that is; yes, and there are tidbits now and then.

I liked very much the way the tamer appeared with a quite unromantic cohort. His attire was simple. For his own amusement, seemingly, he applied the butt end of his whip to the nose of one or the other of his minions, to rouse him up, like a teacher telling his students: "Pay attention now!" Wonderful it is, indeed, physical strength under control on its way to mental endeavor. As for the dangers of this trade, one should try not to exaggerate or underrate them. The tamer put his arms around the wickedest, wildest lion's yellow neck, simply to jest with him. He did so primarily, of course, for the beauty of such display.

One offers the public a sensation so as to retain its interest. But secondly—a lion tamer likes his lions, and best of all he likes the one which has remained most original, the most leonine lion. His chief concern is for the one that gives him most to do. It's the same for a lover with women, a charactered officer with his troops, a father with his children, et cetera. But thirdly, a lion tamer can tell himself, in such a case, that what has come to be compliant, if pressed by need or whim, or by the law of nature, can become nasty, insofar as something nasty, by the law of alternation, provided that one allows it the honor to believe that this is the way things are, is also willing enough to be nice. In any case, the lion tamer must have a high degree of self-confidence as well as confidence in his clients. Every single gesture he makes is absolutely sure. Courage is indispensable. His attitude must show the lions that they won't be doing anything to him: "Nothing can happen to me!" And even if he thinks quite otherwise, he must act as if he were the god of lions. He must be both beautiful and brutal, so as not to make use of his pistol—that would be bad for business.

August 1925: *Prager Presse. SW* 17.

These little services

These little services, of singular loveliness, earlymorningish, and, taken from peaceful sleep, the hint of a gallant century, and no other than the rosy eighteenth. I can hardly give you a ready circumscription of a countess who always rode toward me, as if out of a Watteau, in the forest, mornings, robed in her delicacy. Her horse was crazed with pleasure at being permitted to carry a rider no less beautiful, no less fine, than herself with whom it quietly danced along. By their delight to be spectators of a so tender romantic scene the green leaves were transformed into silver ditties, while little birds were mute with admiration rising to astonishment. O, the dear things, how they could have twittered, had they not been so inhibited, so abashed. Impossible for them to be anything but contented, in bliss and silence. Fool that I am, I supposed the countess to be so tall that her feather hat, which she might have borrowed from the thirteenth century, touched the edge of heaven, I mean its infinitely inviting breath, which is indefinable for us and will probably remain so. She appeared to be longness personified but revealing no fault, no lapse into fragility. I hardly dare touch on the transparency of her glorious velvet gown and the velvet softness of her skin, which remained veiled from my sight. What's more, she wasn't a real countess, she only enjoyed the advantage of hearing herself so called out of this mouth of mine. Seeing her approach from the hall of columns which the spreading woodland seemed to form, herself a very painting, an incarnation of poetry and music, as well as a picture of courtesy, I was surrounded by shadows and luminosities, and into the calmest and deepest lakes of sweet carnality I sank, while at the same time I felt raised aloft to the heights of human mindliness. Naturally I worshiped her, the loveliest, tenderest object anyone can devise. My numerous, indescribably rich, red, blue, and green crazinesses seemed to make me the wisest man on earth, a project before which I set no obstacle whatever. "How can I be of service to you?" I asked, and from up on her horse she replied: "By infusing me with the sense, my boy," for so she was pleased to address me, "enchanting me as it does, that with your big loyal eyes you like to look at me." Isn't that how an utterly heavenly being speaks? My heart leaped to break when she smiled, this miracle from God's workshop. Then I turned deathly pale and for sorrow my head took on a tilt, like a figure in an El Greco, but never was there a felicity to vie with the kiss my sorrow gave. Then away she would float, but on the next day she'd reappear to me, in the same poetically luxuriant place, and the most painful joys and joyous torments, like hanging gardens abrim with inexpressible things, began afresh. The small houses dispersed over the neighborhood acquired, from my very pleasure in them, ruddy cheeks. Nobody endeavored to make it plausible to me that life was not killing, death not beautiful, and love not the supreme task and reward. Meanwhile I didn't hesitate, of course, to type heart-winning letters to supervisory ladies, which I might presume to have been read with the liveliest desire, as must have been the case, for I certainly am an artist whenever the intention allows me that condition and the thought that I have it all suggests itself to me. Yet for the love-deprived who are full of love, who are constantly close to the center of Being and removed from it, something is constantly missing. If I saw her, I did not ever see her as vividly as when she had withdrawn, blinded by the sight of her as I was. O, the joy of her voice! Enough, enough, I'm lost, and that means more than you think. Whoever you are, reading this, I entreat you most passionately not to consider me pitiful, but rather to be envied. We think we must understand each other, but that's quite unnecessary. To be self-sufficient is really much more sensible. Neither obtains anything from the other, if he understands him, but he has much if he's pleased to see him, and is refreshed, if he speaks.

Autumn 1925. *B* 5.

Ramses II

Ramses II became younger with the passing of the centuries. At night he would sleep in tool chests. For a time, people said he lacked talent, yet opinions changed, in view of his immediatenesses. He was by nature extremely slim. With mummies, that much goes without saying. To his thousand-year-old conscience bustling Pastor Künzli spoke in vain. On Ramses impressions made hardly any impression. Pastor Künzli alerted the pharaoh to the expectation that, as assiduously as possible, a decent person should shave. Upon this demand Ramses smiled generously. The smile was somewhat pyramidal. In vain the young farmboys danced around him, he kept his distance from folk art, but without straining himself. Novikoff, this certainly meritorious product of the pusta, tried to instill the art of cracking jokes into the Egyptologist. Ramses II main-tained, in the face of these endeavors, a sphinx-like attitude. Enchanting, his smooth, bald, furbished skull. Sculptors offered him whatever he might ask if he could be moved to stand as a model, but he supported his position with the excuse that he was otherwise occupied. He was not informative as to the nature of such claims on him. His muteness was considered a sight worth seeing. Girls found him very interesting, but shouted out loud that he was boring. Good Pastor Künzli, who seemed much concerned with the salvation of his client's soul, provided him with good books, but the mummy preferred penny dreadfuls, and seemed to show some sophistication in this regard. For a time the story ran that he had revolutionary intentions, but soon it was clear as day that Ramses thought well of his adoptive country. Now and then, with his admittedly rather thin fingers, chiseled almost into invisibility as they were, he wrote, and writing proposed itself to him as an exercise of no small value. A few of these poems were even printed, though Pastor Künzli shook his head over them. Physical jerks, Ramses thought, were especially useful. Novi-koff gave up trying to make a happy fellow out of someone whose face never changed its expression. As for the cleanliness of our subject, it was like freshly fallen snow. This was admitted even by persons who had occasionally hoped he might leave much to be desired in that quarter. Some people said he was a born educator, but he wanted people to know that this was doubtful. He was comfortable with the thought that he was comfortable. Purposefulness of that kind seemed to him pointless. Indeed, his culture was unspoiled. He antagonized educated people, if ever they perceived this. Culture is too sedate, they think, for education rests on activity. Moreover it could be believed that Pastor Künzli was an artist, for he would always walk about in a hat which had a broad and black brim. Ramses could never be persuaded that headgear had its uses. Little girls also, to them his fabulous and unassuming conduct was inevitably deaf. His need to be instructed was generally understood, but he saw in supposed inexperience a stimulus to living. It was out of grandiosity that he made himself small. He banished toothache by most attentively palpating his feet, as if playing the piano. I've heard that he laid a claim to being embraced by the most delicate arms of girls and kissed by the freshest of lips. Indeed a Ramses may claim all sorts of things without needing to fear ridicule. Is there not latent in man's insatiability, in this thronging of wishes, in all this fearful alarm, clamorous, then quietly swimming down into the silence and chasms of the Unfulfilled, something like a laugh? O, for delicacy's sake, better set all such considerations aside. Ramses must be reckoned with, hoped for. This attitude itself might indicate a highly developed understanding. He doubtless assigns to himself a value. At those who laugh at him he laughs, and he commiserates with those who commiserate with him, and people say that he gets up quite early in the morning; and he thinks much, and he thinks nothing. Actually, he doesn't think, no, his thinking thinks. His thoughts buzz around him, encircle him like plaintive, puzzled children, who are exposed and who would like to come indoors, but he is always finding new ones that he cannot retain. This Ramses is, well, quite simply he is a world.

October–December 1925. *B* 5.

Spanish Wine Hall

There in this relatively airy hall we sat, and while from a little stage a dancer showed us her skills, so and so many cigars were lit and so and so often the glass with its heartening contents was lifted to the mouth. The room was, of course, packed, and women sat there laughing all over their faces. Nonetheless a too serious person left because her husband had reproached her for offering no occasion for some fun. It was perhaps quite sensible of her to disappear from a place that served to provide amusement. I had with me a nicely printed and condemned novella. Well, with this production of my mind I now stepped up to a lady who was surrounded by admirers and offered it to her for sale, naming a fairly reckless price. The lady agreed. At once she began to read the novella and it seemed to me that she was satisfied with it, for I saw her smile. Only over persons who are contented comes the urge to curl, prettily, the lips. The dancer received flowers, and from his spouse, who was keeping a watchful eye on him, a too frolicsome husband received an admonitory and affectionate slap, which seemed almost to augment his exuberance. She was such a dainty little woman, and he a real muscle-man type, but precisely such as he are able to appreciate tender chastisements. Out of the forest of faces around me one fräulein's nose stood out, but actually the nose was hanging downward, rather than boldly climbing upward; it seemed to possess a lot of philosophy. The music sounded vigorous and warm, it warmed the chamber like a stove, this stove bubbled with none-too-tuneful tunes. With these tunes it was like this: they formed a boat, or, if you like, a gondola, the listener accordingly sat in it and the gondola glided along, and the person who'd made himself comfortable there could think about something, for example, Spain.

While thinking now about Spain, I recalled Lesage's novel, entitled *Gil Blas*, which was written during the seventeenth century in Paris, and the whole carpet of it unrolls in Spain, because for a long time it was the custom for all novels to be set in the land of bull fighting. Anyone unacquainted with that novel is missing something quite beautiful and educative, for the language in which the book is written is most pleasing. I thought of Spanish cities like Barcelona and Madrid, Granada and Seville, which were once partly under Arab sovereignty and could be Christianized only step by step, so to speak. Could anyone versed in literature not know the graceful, heartfelt, sweet, jolly poem by Brentano, in which the most fetching girls of Seville peep out from the windows? Is not the world-famous Don Juan a thoroughly Spanish figure? As regards painting, how resounding they are for us, the names of best significance: Velasquez painted the most solemn court jesters, Goya the most captivating courtesans. The landscape of Spain is beautiful, or so I was assured by someone with whom I had a conversation about courtesy, which is also at home, as it were, in Spain. It is a very important cultural medium. I consider courtesy to be just as right as honesty, or almost more important than it, for honesty often upsets us. I thought of Beaumarchais and Mérimée, those Frenchmen who were enthusiastic about Spain.

Meanwhile the lady had drawn on her gloves. Seeing her prepare to leave the wine hall, I stood up, so that she'd look at me in a fitting manner, that is, with respect. There was something Figaro-like about the attitude I adopted toward her, I mean a complacent air. Approvingly she took note of my endeavor to show her that I was in good spirits. When she'd left, a breath of genteel irony existed in the place no longer, but I alone noticed this, my nerves being alert to everything. The proprietor was busy, just as he'll have liked to be. As for me, I made that evening an acquaintance as unimportant as it was nice, lovely, slight, subtle, and, I believe, appropriate.

November 1925: *Berliner Tageblatt. SW* 17.

It can so happen that

It can so happen that, for example, horses are unduly put to work, because they cannot speak and thus cannot be asked. They are unable to negotiate. No horse can be asked for its opinion, for nature has denied it the ability to pronounce one. It is altogether disgusting the way human beings do not refuse such delicacies as frogs' legs. Without more ado, day in and day out unnumbered heads are chopped off chickens in the civilized world, a fact that should give pause for thought. Thinking herself a benefactress, a woman came home one day with a live eel, she wanted to serve it to me for luncheon. But from the task of killing the eel she shrank. "Won't you, dear friend, accomplish the murder?" she asked me. Out of kindness I then took up my singular task, making every effort to master my nerves—and succeeding. Hens lay eggs and in gratitude for this concession we butcher them, eat them, too. On the one hand, it's really useful, on the other it's ruthless. Meanwhile alimentation, a matter of eminent magnitude, does have to be considered. With an intelligent glance or two around, one sees how the animals must sacrifice them-selves to human appetite. The animals are raised artificially in order to be exterminated, or they are fed so as to be enlisted in occupations. Geese, ducks, and the rest, what wickedness have they perpetrated, that some-one should kill them? The offense of these creatures is to be edible, to some extent even delicacies for us insatiable beings, who are quick and happy to decorate ourselves with the Medal of Humanity. If every con-sumer of meat-soups, every abolisher of veal chops had to assist with the killing required for his alimentation, he might occasionally perhaps lose his appetite. For us, what we don't see might as well not have happened, which explains some of the thoughtlessness of people, for example, who stayed at home during the world war. So now I'll speak of war and beg to be allowed to say that no one war is like another, that every war is indeed something nobody would wish for, but that for us Europeans, for example, there may arise a need to wage war in our culture's interest, meaning against colonial peoples, who, disposed as they are and as things are with us, absolutely have to do what we tell them to do. Toward some protests to the contrary one can be indulgent, others will have to be thoroughly subdued, tamed. So one shouldn't blindly condemn all wars, rather one must earnestly ask what aim, what purpose a war has. The colonial peoples are under European supervision, on them has been laid the obligation to conform, as precisely and wisely as possible, to our intentions, needs, and so forth. It would be near-madness for them to misunderstand an order in which, as *Naturvölker*, they have had to accept a subordinate role. Of course, one can't insist on this, and I'm not insisting on anything, only presuming. If the animals must sacrifice themselves for the continuance of humanity, then one may make the same demand of human beings. As no one war is like another, so one man is not the same as another. The condition of peace, if it is to prosper, requires immense resources. People who think and talk emotionally seldom ponder this issue with sufficient concentration. Besides, in the interest of peace, I would counsel, or advise, that it not be taken as an exclusive configuration or object of thought, because I believe there arises from thinking along such a continuum a fervid atmosphere, one that is indeed a threat to peace. One recalls how, time and again, as one might say, a certain person with the world's most powerful fighting resources at his disposal, declared that his mission was to guarantee the peace. Legend tells us to reflect that serpents lurk under the flowers. Can a war be of any use to us? Today things are so constellated that I do not venture to answer at all such an unspeakably hard question, a question of such unspeakably fine-ground hardness, such a glittering black diamond of a question. I'd like only to have raised it. It is my opinion, my feeling, my conviction that one must have the courage to ask oneself this question, for I think nothing so harmful as catchwords whose meanings can turn, imperceptibly slowly but absolutely, in the hush of their clockwork progression, into their opposites. At the mere word "war" one shouldn't shiver and show a squeamish distaste, one should look this word, this concept, straight in the eye, like a lion that means to hurt us, and that we must fend off, must subdue. On the nature of peace and war some marvelous deep words, words so remarkable that they might be likened to abysses, were put by Miguel Cervantes, who knew war at first hand and had reflected upon it, into the mouth of his Don Quixote de la Mancha, on the occasion of a banquet. There the foolish but wholly magnanimous and philanthropic knight said that peace springs from war and the latter from the former, and he declared that it was war that brought peace, but he had the tact not to declare this as if he were a lover whose viciousness rolls away from him like a golden, shimmering, gleaming little ball from the palm of his hand and who smiles a fine snaky rhetoric out of his mouth, and whose eyes gaze without misgiving, in all innocence. Perhaps those were not his words and perhaps I'm inventing a bit here, for which I beg pardon. Anyway, the Spanish writer's words, which he places on the lips of a madman who behaved at times with the greatest good sense, challenge us to think deeply. Sometimes innocence and harmlessness can really be self-deceiving. Let us never overlook that. The best intentions have to be fearlessly monitored. Let us not for a moment forget that we are mechanisms, parts in a divine structure that is in many ways a complete puzzle to us. From this one must not shrink. As regards everything that has happened, however, I think it more proper, more wise, more profitable, more appealing, now and then to lose our faith, our confidence in ourselves; they will not perish if we do so. Trust and mistrust do constitute one identity in the person whose mind is awake. For us it is advisable to admit that our understanding of our own concerns could be mistaken, mistaken our view of our surroundings. If with prayer and supplication we could only attract to ourselves whatever we want, everything would be quite simple. But if this is not the way things are done, it's still a beautiful gesture. As I see it, the gesture contains something salutory for us. With prayer it is certainly not a matter of succeeding, of accomplishing something useful, but first and foremost of its being beautiful.

February–March 1926. *B* 4.

Brentano (III)

Brentano was writing: I and a few others of my stamp have rushed ahead of the times we're drifting around in like birds in a cage, nervously knocking our wings against the bars. My ebony curls make fun of me. Sometimes they seem like leaden slates loading me down. Ironclad ships plough quietly and grandly through the sea of my far-off imaginings, and in every idea there's truth and every emotion eats itself up, and this cubbyhole here is dark, like a poor, shy, tiny heart, and imprisoned in their agility my hands are blithe, desperate dancing girls, and flowers on tall stalks gaze, as if with large eyes, into this trap I've accustomed myself to calling "room." As if muttering, as if suffering, the curtain stirs a little, and prayers speed across the mountains, which seem spellbound, and here on the desk is a letter from a girl who loves to stroll about in men's clothes and tells me her father has bought her a castle in the middle of an oak forest, and she tells me she's waiting for me, so as to have company when she feels like taking a walk through the greenery with its thousand shivering, trembling, sparkling interruptions, she is captivatingly slim, so she says, and she expresses the hope that I have in mind a lot of games and jokes, like objects neglected, charming, feather-stippled, in a box, so one would only have to extract them, one after another. She says her castle is most strangely set up, with an abundance of hideyholes, half temple, half palace, and, inbetween, something like a hunting lodge; also it's a bit weathered already, like a delicate, beautiful, pious woman somehow come down in the world, who displays nevertheless quite clearly, balm for every soul, a noble lineage.

But while I'm reading this letter, written by a lady who doesn't love me but only feels me to be an entertaining person with whom she's taken it into her head to pass away the time, there rises before me, sickly, edged with mournful black, the black and golden thought of the purple-yellow flaming sunflower, such being my name for the bourgeoise I believed I could carry up to heaven when I climbed at night into her room, lifted her out of bed and carried her away in my brown arms; and who now, to put it coolly, is in difficulties, as I am, too, on her account. I thought I was strong, the warmest, most obliging model of dependability, whereas now and then the fancy seizes me that early every morning I should be going to school again, for a precociously flowering haste to enter time and life has flung me back upon the wish, oddly and also simply, to begin my existence afresh.— Therefore times come when I cannot possibly take life seriously, because planted deep in me is a blithe belief that life is only a delightfully helpless child, watched over by a mother's eyes, lying in the playful, lush-green, yielding grass. Soft flames try to lick their way out of me, to dominate me, and I feel akin to swallows or snowflakes; then again before me stands, full-grown, all the responsibility.

Bettina is like me but she has the advantage of being a girl, allowed to wind herself around men who are just and intelligent, whereas the man in me rebels against my essentials, on which subject he is understandably not to be consulted. What a gentle and angry instrument I am, and I talk, and in all the talk there expands a steppe of speechlessness, and I can be silent, and something in that silence raises a continual shout. I don't love the world, yet I love it. If I had my way, all the highways would be carpeted and from every mouth every utterance would be a caress. My really very beautiful, subtle hands love me, like female devotees who have too pretty a conception of the object of their zeal. I use them for writing poems, grasping door-handles, pulling bell-ropes, washing and combing, and for shaking other hands, as custom requires. If I walk around at night my face comes into contact with a confusion of hanging branches. Frivolous people think me frivolous, serious people serious, but all that ever happens is that I bring relief to the deeply thoughtful, yet make the happy hang their heads. People who are suffering become frolicsome in my presence, guilty ones I make innocent, and serpents of guilt slither round the innocent; I kill something in those who are lively, and with the music-making and balm of my interest I strengthen the weak, and sickly people take courage at the thought of my existence, and with my questioning looks I make the healthy pensive, the paths that pass through the beauties and infamies and sanctities and darknesses and freedoms and captivities of existence blanch when they see me, only to glow at once with gratification, and the houses stand there, and in the cities it is clearly to be seen how people yearn for love and how difficult this was, yesterday as well as today. They never yield, the obstacles we make, they endure, they are resilient. From the possibilities hang rags, as from beggarfolk. And yet one likes to catch sight of them.

It seems to me that education passed over me too quickly, and that I did not often enough take a stand, so as to make use, on occasion, of what I had acquired. As regards education, I confess to believing that use enhances it. The clock ticks. The little garden is like someone of whom one is thinking. Voices are to be heard. Whether it's cold or warm, day or night, people are always on the move, except in sleep, but even there they are breathing. Tomorrow evening I'm supposed to read verses at a social gathering; I shall have to master my restlessness and revive a habit, and people will smile at what touches them too deeply, and at any exuberance they will think it proper to grimace somewhat.

April 1926: Prager Presse. SW 17.

From the Life of a Writer

Turning one might catch sight here and there of the glowing red of a woman's hat, and then of the shimmering white tremor of a birch tree's trunk. The color paramount at this time of the year is, naturally, green, which makes sometimes a soft, sometimes a loud sound, and each accordingly, with a special quality, issues an invitation apparently familiar, yet again fresh. The green of fields differs from that of trees. And you, now, can you never be seen? Altogether, you seem to have retired from your occupation of being visible and perceptibly kind.

O, what tulip sounds, red and blue, leaped, rang, and fell upon my ear from a villa unknown to me this morning at about eleven thirty, as if someone I could not see stood in a room inside and tossed me a spellbinding gift. As it happened, someone indoors was playing a piano. To judge by the touch it could have been a girl, the "daughter of the house." When music is being played indoors and chance, or that which is so called, leads me past, I like it extraordinarily. It is the surprise that I like about such bourgeois practices. With a head full of thoughts flitting into the mind's eye, out again, and in again, one comes from somewhere, then suddenly fingers galloping over the keyboard, or, as in a boat, gliding over the calm lake of such an instrument, bring a pleasant hello. Should you not then shout inwardly for joy like an apprentice to experience, for whom life is still rather strange?

Even if one is restored and refreshed enough, the lady, music by name, admonishes—that the errant soul is what one is; and she reminds one, excessive luxury though this may seem, that it is pleasing to be consoled. As a doctor lifts the dressing from a patient's wound, to examine its condition, she lifts from our seclusions, as it were, a lid. For in a sense we all have wounds, though customarily we overlook this sensitive fact, which daily existence covers up, so no wound is in evidence.

Yesterday I saw a horseman chase through a countryside exploding with primaveral verdure, and if I'd brought a lute along, on my Sunday walk that led me past an imposing château I'd once, so and so many years ago, "patrolled" as a recruit, I would have joyously sung out across the treetops, to the solitary, beautiful cinquecento edifice, some such words as "Behind which casement seekest thou, angel, thy repose?" Of course, I'd have recited the words in the form of a poem, and village girls would have come by and with great marveling eyes gazed for a long time upon the wayfaring journalist and minstrel, curious to know who he was and whence he came.

For eight hours I walked yesterday, my landlady having told me how little she appreciated a lodger who did nothing but sit at home and write sketches such as this one might be.

Back in the town, pinks were fragrant, along with productions of the mind in bookshops. Here I stood facing red globes; they were Dutch cheeses. Exclusively ladies' stockings were displayed in a shop window. I nipped smartly into a coffee shop behind two beautiful unknowns in the shape of females, and in their proximity, to my delight, I stayed a while.

Bodies, the garments for which are charming because they overlay charms, and which one loves because they envelop lovelinesses and softly move with every supple motion of the body, lucky things they are, the garments women wear, for I consider them (O, the idea of a schoolboy) lucky and sheltered, permitted as they are to decorate what they shelter.

Words have a life, so has merchandise, so has work, and in each sensibility meanings assemble, and the laughing proprietress of every country tavern is yet another testimony to existence declaring itself everywhere. Walking along the country road I discussed with myself the meaning of marriage; I was unable to appreciate it to its advantage, that is, in the interest of its viability. An appreciation is always accompanied by a depreciation, and the latter, too, is important, because everything is important.

It's a pleasure to say that I saw, at an exhibition, the self-portrait of a great painter, and, posted on a pillar, the announcement of a famous play forthcoming. The portrait had heart; the play—study as I may, I can find no word to suit it, but that's no reason to be annoyed with myself.

At present I'm reading a most tastefully written novel.

I'm more active than seems to be the case.

The first impression I make on myself is one of being wide awake, a satisfactory state, reason enough to think I'm capable of something.

May 1926: *National-Zeitung, Basel. SW* 18.

Letter of a European

I'm at present in such a purified and peaceful state. The soul in me even seems too harmonious. I'm almost amazed. I read newspapers, because the many importunate books tell you what you already know. I find the papers poetic, because they inform me about realities. Something in me tells me not to fantasize, or at least advises me to refrain from doing so. And I do not fantasize about you, for I consider that a sin, and here I am, writing to you now, confessing coincidentally that I have a relationship with a woman who has a high regard for me and presides over a flock of ladies in her service, who thus can hardly be called ladies, and servants would be a more deserving title. Very fond of me as this woman is, you will hardly venture to hold that against me, well, I mean you may so venture, but would something that pleases me and doesn't trouble you do any good or harm? Excuse, I ask you, the candor of these words. I'm not a person you are longing for, it's true, but here's what I wanted to talk about: I've an inclination nowadays toward Europeanry.

You may in future regard me as a genuine, that is, unequivocal, European, and if we should ever engage in a discussion, you'll have the honor of conversing with a person who has read, for instance, Anatole France, of whom you do not perhaps know that cultivated people hold him in high esteem, because he was a pronounced friend to mankind.

Currently I'm living in a European way and in comfort, that's to say, in a room which, if endowed with the faculty of speech, would ask to be designated as a "drawing room." The apartment is, however, silent, all day the windows are open, I hear the clatter of hoofs shod with iron, it's so cosy, and then I wanted to tell you that to me you're still a dear person, though actually it's improper for a master of all his parts to make tender protestations. On my desk lie the writings of important authors. My cupboards are high, not that they lack the corresponding dimension of depth: there I can tidily keep everything that flows from my pen, until I sell it to a taker, who is occasionally happy when at a sensible price I surrender to him what I have written. Many poems have been written about you, for of all thinkable persons you are the foremost, and you play a principal role in publications. Whether you like this I cannot know, because we have never had an opportunity to speak together. Yet generally what I've printed about you can hardly displease you, though by some descriptions you might have been a touch mispleased, considering how I imagine the pleasure that in principle I alone understand. Persons loved are sometimes unable to penetrate the realm of joy of those who are lovingly devoted to them, and, for sure, the lovers are much, much more fortunate than those who are loved, as will be obvious to you, I think, without more being said.

I've become, as I told you, much quieter. Once I did disquieten you with my disquiet. You looked upon me as upon a forest hemming you in with its thickets, but I'd like to believe that now the forest has been thinned, and I mean my temperament, which nowadays resembles a nicely wallpapered sitting room, whereas, at the time of our encounters, it was more undesirably like a moonlit attic. In those days I hadn't yet moved up into the reception of Europeandom. For then I often behaved toward you in rather uncivilized ways; and, that said, I stand before you as one asking forgiveness, without being so lacking in taste as to waste words. Yet how lovely it is that all this time I could serve you like your cavalier, for a long time never asking your permission; that's to say, I've written and set before the public a little book, in which you are sitting, as it were, on a bench under leaves that whisper around you, which befriend you, leaf by leaf, and wish you all the happiness that the enthusiastic writer does. You cannot imagine the extent and the sincerity of the enthusiasm you aroused in me; and I never expect you to bother about it, either—that would be too onerous a task. Chivalry forbids me to require you to comprehend how I courted you, to grasp the degree to which I, yes, adored you, although that word does have a somewhat trivial ring.

At that time my most intense desire was to be able to kiss you; because this wish was not fulfilled, I withdrew into "seclusion," let all the tenderness, while feeding the idea that such tenderness was a child you would not heed, flow into the lines I wrote so as to be occupied, and then those lines found their way to cultivated persons, by whom they were read. Of course, nobody knows who you are, and you can certainly imagine how very careful I was to observe discretion while at my occupation, and at present I don't yet know if I shall post this letter, for despite all my friendship with you there is a voice that unceasingly warns me against you, telling me—I can't believe I've heard it said—that you are vengeful and utterly without love for me, that you mean to shame me, are not adequately disposed, not prepared to respect me, rather your one concern is in one way or another to confuse me. How glad I'd be if this does you an injustice, how gladly I'd be entitled, before the judges of culture, to believe in you like a child, and indeed I do so, but there are people who have certain ideas in these matters, these people have reputations, the opinions of these reputable people must be considered, and here I come back to Europeandom, of which I count myself a member, perhaps unjustifiably, but that's how it goes, even if one can hardly think it possible, and to such a European as I am today some things that an irresponsible and harmless joker may undertake, are not permitted. So nowadays I'm not quite so harmless as before, and I feel myself bound, in one way or another, and my eyes can shine up to you only on condition that you know who I am, that you know I represent a value. I wish, in a word, to be respected. Even lovers have nowadays thus their dignity, and I speak here simply the language of the times in which I live and I will never kiss anyone unless I've kissed you first, yet even then I'll never kiss you, unless you, too, step out as a European.

If you wish to help this along, then be so kind as to tell the one who can only kiss you in a good European way, which means honorably, for the moment has come when no loyal and passionate person is free to act demeaningly, and he feels that he stands in the forum of an alliance with all others, that is, in society, with a duty to declare himself, for he is resolved to reveal at all times what is in his mind. I'm sorry, very sorry about writing this; I, too, regret that nobody belongs any more exclusively to himself. For a long time to come we must watch out for one another. That it came to this is a pity. Who now can claim to have a cheerful heart? I'll ask all sorts of clever people how far a heart can go in being heartful. You'll be so kind as to be patient for a while, for I don't doubt that you are a dear person, and doubt just as little that I, too, am one, though you don't see it yet. Today nobody has any right to show joy with all candor. Just think how many are sick—if I may permissibly remind you. How could the gap have arisen between us, how can it possibly be closed? I'd like for once to see you do a good thing. Who now is good? Who has the courage to do good? One thing I ask of you: waste no effort on trying to impress me, for, if you did, then I, too, would seem to be what I am not, and of that there have been many instances. All this is so paltry. Kissing and loving in these times, nobody can consider them more than marginal, merely a gift to us, and who will not love the great remindings, which are no pleasure?

May 1926: Berliner Tageblatt. SW 17.

O how in this not large

O how in this not large, not too spacious but stylishly maintained, discreet, somehow imposing palace on the lake, on the seashore, the river, or the brook, intellectually eminent men, monks, one would like to say, brotherly cloistral cohabitants, relished baked fish and demolished it with a propriety most exquisite. The house, or the mansion, was a kind of pleasance or convalescent home for medieval devotees of culture. The proceedings were once, so it seems, in equal measure lordly and thin-blooded, festive and solemn. Up the slope ran the vines, and the one thing these knew was benignly to dispense the wine that later, at appropriate intervals, bubbled and shone in the glass, and flowed down through the veins into the being of the drinkers. By skiff or gondola or rowboat they rowed across the calm, golden lake-surface to an island not far distant, which appeared to some of them perhaps like a paradise, because it was so large, so beautiful, so inviting and welcoming, like a lady's hat, green in summer, yellow and red in the autumn, with its elegant brim spread to the water, which seemed to touch it, kissing it with its lips, and to moisten it, this hat. On the island there was another cloistral abode of art and morals, and on the shore of the lake there smiled, pastoral, farmerly and agriculturally, the separate villages, and everything in those days went along so merrily. The lake was known far and wide as a waterway, a trade route. Deeply buried Byzantine coins were found here recently, proof of earlier mercantile endeavors and fiscal conditions and far wanderings from the Orient to the Western world. Perhaps Greek empresses trailed, at repose on splendid ships, their glorious imperial hands in the delicate, subtle, indulgent water, letting themselves be caressed by its soft, sweet, cooling mouth, as they traveled over this prettily yet grandly shaped lake, which, for any who go there, seems to lead to a land of the sagas, the domain of fairytales. For here there did exist, full of brisk activity and aspiration, towns that have meanwhile entirely disappeared, as if they had never sparkled with towers and battlements and windowpanes and greeted and flapped with pennons and standards and never from the city hall steps proclaimed peace and other treaties and trumpeted their ordinances. Then came a time when the lakeside palace was used for the purpose of overlordship, as a family took possession of it. Many a good, readable book, composed and written perhaps by Wildenbruch or some other fertile writer, was read undisturbed in the garden, the quiet garden, which extends from the façade down to the inland water, of which we think enough has been said. Evenings, no doubt, the daughters would practice études on the piano, a thing, I ask, not to be understood ironically, since voyagers, gypsying folks, wanderers, as they walked by on the road, would certainly have been rejoiced by the sensitive figures and over the keys the gliding of fingers, slender fingers, on which glittered a ring, which might be an engagement ring, and so continued on their way with fresh courage, touched by the faery hand of confidence in experiences yet to come. Today the house has become an inn, which is apparently profitable, of which at least profitability is assumed. Everything has to legitimize itself by profitability nowadays. Legitimate is the outlay, for example, the bearing of interest, the punctual covering of expenditures, combined with profit. I heard the novel of this old-time house, which I have rendered as concisely and in as general a tone as possible, from the laughing mouth of a girl who, for a year or longer feeling herself almost a patrician, had lived in one of the numerous delightful rooms that the building contains, with a view like a shining showcase and far-reaching as [. . .]

Summer 1926. *B* 4.

Apparently not a cloud was to be seen

Apparently not a cloud was to be seen up there, or one might just as well
say down there. I remember staying in that region for three months, or
perhaps only two weeks, or might it have been a stay of three weeks? My
excellent memory declines to supply the information, but not to an-
nounce to you, with what amounts to certainty, that, yes, there it appeared
impossible for nature not to show to man a cloudless countenance, and
her rivers and her rocks shone like an inviting, affectionate smile. In the
region of which I'm telling, the river was in a juvenile condition, a
condition, so to speak, of eternally beautiful, eternally meaningful nov-
elty, and if its conduct was unruly, it had the welcome stamp of childlike-
ness. Moreover, insofar as a God has been announced to us, of whom it
can be said, can be believed, that he exists everywhere, occurs everywhere,
rules everywhere, I'd be inclined to find life tolerable everywhere, for
people like me have the good fortune, I mean almost good genius, to
possess a homeland with no limits, but let me revert to my favorite region,
where constructed on crags there were gardens consisting of plantations
of trees, whose leaves, in their shape and toning, could match for elegance
and delicacy any in the world, and between them the peaches and apricots
could peep coquettishly out, that is, with promise of joy, as if their foliage
were maidenhair and their fruits the eyes belonging to faces no one could
help but love on first sight, by which I only mean to stress that they found
one's approval instantly. Where this country, or neck-of-the-woods, is, I'd
therefore rather not tell, otherwise everything on two legs would travel
and leap and rush and walk thither, disconcerting it with curiosity, which
usually has nasty and noxious results. O, to see there in the evening how
those evenings, with their folksinging atmosphere, so enveloped the grey
old walls of lofty, most gracefully and precisely built castles, that one sank
plummeting into a rapturous world-historical deep thought as into a
sumptuous bed and saw cuirassed and sword-bearing characters out of

long-performed and oft-seen plays and elegant heroic figures, crowned with wit and the best of attitudes, floating before one's hearkening and receptive soul. The clear blue morning was always like, how should I say, a generous promise from a goddess with a mouth of gold, a mouth that seemed equally remote from truth and falsehood, seemed unable to lie, because it was, itself, truth's instrument, which then was unable, nor ever needed, to tell a truth, because truths for it were of a concept too brief, too small, and too cramping. It was no other than nature herself of whose lips I speak, of whose mountains I declare to you that, like the skylark, that is, mountainously embodying the delight, the high delights of skylarks (their eternal snow no ostentation, since they take it for granted), they soared into the air. If they lacked wings and seemed to flutter and fly, if they glowed like flames of stone, that will have been due to a certain moderation of theirs, akin to the utmost immoderation. In any case they were uniquely there for valleys to assume their shapes, with floral meadows carpeting them most pleasantly, over which shepherds and shepherdesses strolled as it behooved them, not overmuch troubling about the flocks entrusted to their keeping, since they knew them to be well accommodated. Were not the churches in the towns and villages of this region like pious women in regulation dress and bells tolling an expression of the destiny of all the women, in love and in life, and what could be for me more proper and apposite than to presume to persuade myself that it would really be very nice for me to mention the graves of early Christians, over whose subsidence, preceded by the weariness they could not forfend, being not bodies of bronze but transient ones, later the figures emerged who could number themselves among the purified, that is, civilized, down from whose towers, like soft- and large-plumed birds carrying ribbons with the inscription LOVE in their sacred beaks, the trumpets instituting union blared as far as the sea, which people in this clime think to be near, although with these words I've certainly not wanted to roll out anything but the characterization of a landscape, of which I would ask most humbly that from the limits of its frame, of a common cultural bond, it be not extracted, though that has in my opinion often been done with the endeavors of a writer such as I am, as if I had something in mind, something unseemly, that would never have occurred to me, far from any such thing as I always knew myself to be. Who's to blame that I must defend myself, instead of carrying on in company with a trust that people expect some good of me?

Autumn 1926. *B* 4.

The White Lady

Last night I was returning from an excursion that had taken up a good twenty hours, it was three in the morning, when in the stillness of the night I saw a figure standing motionless by a pillar, but I'll be coming back to this later.

There's a certain impertinent face I'll endure no longer. What am I talking about? For the present I prefer not to say. Apposite explanations will surely follow, I promise; so, to proceed.

O, Othello, how far were you driven? I don't understand specifically why the name of a stage character should spring to my lips, which tremble theatrically as I mention a lover who was too passionate.

There exists a friendly kind of conduct that is, in effect, arrogant. I allude in that sentence to the face just courteously adduced, of the expression on which I seem to have had enough. A colleague's face, perhaps? Quite possibly! For the moment I prefer to talk a bit more about jealousy, which is black as night. Pitch black as bad luck.

I still don't dare to speak at any length about the nocturnal figure already referred to and distinguished by its completely motionless posture. The pleasure I'd known on my walk, I must add, was now gloriously enlarged. An electric light shone down from a mountain peak into the vale, like a pearl on the brow of a worldling girl.

A poetic comparison, I feel it. All the more emphatically, calmly, and with all the more firm a voice, which has, I'm hoping, the requisite mellowness, an undertone of courtesy allied, to some extent, with an overtone of energy, I can now continue this perhaps frivolous, I mean unpremeditated and short, story, and with gratification confirm or assert that a lecturer addressing the greater public unveiled a not in the least disadvantageous portrait of me, presenting me to his audience as an enfant terrible. Amid the ranks of seats I sat, solemnly listening to the address and for decency's sake I kept quiet, which is to say that I acquiesced to that very interesting kind of description, considering that this was the best thing to do.

But that face full of a generous, fine insolence I simply will not accept. It seems that the owner of this evidently sophisticated countenance is bound to apologize to me, as long as he musters the strength to assume a different one. Not for a moment do I doubt that he will. Might I rightly suspect, or believe, or suppose that people designated as cultivated were somehow making fun of the conduct of the so-called uncultivated, while for their part the latter refreshed and braced themselves by contact with the former? Perhaps a sort of reciprocal invigoration occurs, which would certainly be welcome.

How curiously awkward she was, how angular, standing there, that doubtless cultivated, nocturnal, white lady! As a wanderer striding down from the mountains, naturally I had no fear of the apparition, at most, how should I say, a modicum of respect mingled with sympathy. Who was she? Did she have something to tell me? In relation to the figure's height, the head seemed to me surprisingly small. The outstretched hand was completely covered by the spread of her garment—picturesque, I liked that.

But now, reader, get ready for a scene of horror. This morning, merely by putting on an artificially constructed smile feigning cheerful superiority, I pushed an adversary, who perhaps deep down held me in high esteem, into a state of the most total extinctitude. He dropped dead, never to rise again.

The struggles for existence that go on and on, so that streets and squares may be decked out with Renaissance trumpery! The white figure in the night is and remains for me, happily, I might have said, a puzzle.

Before I rose from my couch, or bed, it might have struck five in the morning, I was thinking deeply about literature, and about the possibility of phantom apparitions, and especially about chivalry, toward which we owe our duties today as at all times. However, I did conjecture that these duties have their limits, and was feeling fully satisfied by the results of my meditation. I declared man in general and woman duty-bound to Humanity.

A photograph seen by chance somewhere showed me a husband beside his pretty wife. I mention in passing that he gave me the impression of suffering from a certain distinguished likeness to Othello. I resolve to wriggle most confidently in future through the swarm they call the Public. How sorry I am for the poor white lady!

Fellow citizens, shall we not for a change, in regard to the matter of sharing, try to be both—parsimonious and lavish, thrifty and extravagant; and shall we not, after twelve in the night, when the town is like a fairy picture, and when the soul it was my endeavor to profile meets us, advance toward her with the humble inquiry as to how we might render service to her, for it could be the soul of Europe, perhaps even the World Soul, motionless there, not willing to walk any more.

November 1926: Prager Presse. SW 18.

The Red Thread

Throughout world history, to which I've recently given some attention, there runs like a red thread, even if what I propose may seem at first glance peculiar, a sort of watchword, "I want," which could be personified as a beautiful adventuress with an aigrette in her hair, an elegant riding whip in her gloved hand, traversing on horseback the Plains of Event, History itself, and this—as I gladly admit—quite randomly or fatefully spoken word can only be female. It is recognized that the first of the twain begins, to this writer's great convenience, in the most wholly welcome, because most felicitous, place there ever has been, Paradise, where conceivably the first woman might have said to the first man:

"Be there, if for anything, then for my every satisfaction."

Whereupon the first man, it may be supposed, will have smiled a gentle paradisiac smile and with problematic profundity answered: "I will try to make much of myself."

How to conceive of Paradise, in which everyone is welcome to believe, or how to picture, more or less, its appearance, is a question to which it might be quite difficult to provide an adequate answer. Evidently it has seemed possible to maintain that in its garden, coiled round its trees, a serpent of not inconsiderable size was present, which saw to it that both of the first people were expelled from their condition of felicity, and which chased them out into the wide world doted with a knowledge requisite for the clearly troublesome journey, a gift whose significance did rather little to please its recipients. Sighing bitterly they told one another: "Now we are proletarians who see before them the unpleasant task of earning, by painful exertions, the daily bread which till now, in the form of sweet fruits, dropped into our laps from the good-natured trees."

Indeed, with the departure of the first pair of lovers or friends from an extraordinary abundance of pleasant things, there begins the real movement of world history, of which it cannot be said that it is easy to describe. Can it be maintained that in the loss of Paradise what is called Energy actually originates, and that by a forfeit an advantage was gained, a conquest, specifically the quite rapidly resulting acquisition of the will to life, that is to say, the strength to take up and to carry through, with success or without it, all the troubles and distresses of a struggle? Whichever way one is inclined to feel or think about this, one thing is quite certain: that from the first earnest steps into the cultural or gainful life to the first performance of Mozart's *Don Giovanni* mankind must have sped through the boudoirs at a rate bordering on enormity, such that a glimpse into the sequence would make anyone dizzy, for a person so interested would need to spread his concentrated attention across five parts of the inhabited globe at the same time. My opinion is that for the observer of an almost unsurveyable process it matters little whether one allows eight thousand or eight hundred thousand years for its passage, since more or fewer years affect in no wise the conjecture that man has seen himself submit to developments that he has been more and more pressed to love, whether or not he has had in his heart a great desire to do so. It will have happened that he loved life, because life wanted, utterly, to be glorified by him.

In the belief that he was working his way up out of enslavement and so on, he erected, on the model of Christ, churches and administrative buildings, aspirations that could of course be only slowly, piece by piece, accomplished, for they were mounted on, amongst other things, a huge intruding fact, the exploding of the rock of Paganism. Setting aside the extremely horrifying and disturbing certainty that long before the origination of any human beings there was on earth a life whose only living feature was the earth itself, where soft, tall-boled forests played their lonely colossal symphonies, which no music-lover will have heard, where stone blocks shifted their sedentary or standing locations and, at most, in due course, here and there a dragon, or whatever else it might have wished to be called, stuck its antediluvian head out from a lethargic swamp, it must be a pleasure for me to show my spectator of world history into an era where, with inconceivable velocity, tribal peoples sprouted as if straight from the ground, something that seems today to be strangely not the case, perhaps indeed because a stage in development has been attained that has brought the peoples, diverse as they may well be, to a provisional halt, advising them to be relatively contented with the

71

juncture at which they stopped. As one follows the career of such an attractive object as man, it is his desire for art and for civilization that acquires undeniable significance, in a nutshell the pleasure he takes in liberating himself from all constraints, vexations, or impediments to his delight in existing. Thus, for instance, the gradual emergence of the Christian church signifies for me neither more nor less than an advance along the path of liberation, upon which I just now permitted myself to remark. That the tenth or eleventh century should have ushered numerous fortresses into view, together with ladies and gentlemen and their teams of servants, not only alters nothing in what I've said, but proves the point conclusively, for it was a sheer delight in freedom, nothing else, that moved those who gaily and wilfully gazed down into the valleys, and who had built, with towers and parapets, castles laughing and teeming with the joy of life, from which, with respect to the provision of beautiful dwellings where morals and gaiety could prosper, no applause, least of all the longest and strongest, should be withheld.

In the history of *Bildung*, culture, or the increasing education of man, what is called the court plays a leading role, and this not only in Europe but equally elsewhere, as voyages of discovery, which could only succeed if manifold difficulties were overcome, did luminously show, or, putting it more plainly, verify. What had hitherto been a unifying blessing began in the course of time to go to seed in protracted vexations, by which I mean the disunity that convulsed an association whose merits I have duly considered above. It seems indisputable that the concept of conquest and the idea of freedom become almost indistinguishable, insofar as even the voyages of discovery going out in all directions can have been neither more nor less than travels and journeys toward some liberation or other. Didn't, at one time, the Europeans endeavor, with extraordinary persistence, to liberate the holy places? In other masses of movement, earlier or later, I cannot but discern the red thread by which I was guided when I began to consider this motif, reflection on which certainly in no way allows me to cease from glancing with solicitude into so-called everyday concerns.

I spoke of only touching on matters of an ever-expanding scope, and at the audacity with which I've written these lines on matters of great magnitude I must almost wonder, so that, all unbidden, the position I adopt is one of tact.

1926–27. SW 19.

I would like to be standing

I would like to be standing perhaps today once more at the edge of a little
wood that looks down over a none too splendid village. Years ago I used
to visit now and then that charming spot. Conscious as I am that I wasted
time on that hill, legging it (how else?) into the undergrowth and soon
out again, today I again have a desire to take no account of the costliness
of time. The little village, which lies at the foot of the field and the wood
and the hill and the corn, and which is planted on the rise, certainly
possessed even in those days a character one could approve of, and today,
though its sights should not be overrated, I'd gladly take another look at
it, mainly because of a cottage there, dating from the epoch that saw
Genius flourish and founder, which looked on while highly gifted and
strong individuals gradually had to learn to despair of their gifts and
strengths. Indeed, there are places that waken in us feelings of Storm
and Stress, just as, on the other hand, desolate landscapes can give one
the illusion of standing and walking and eating, sleeping and speaking, in
an epoch of heroes. For sure, heroes had a meager portion of culture,
whereas we tell ourselves, whenever we consider the Stormers and Stress-
ers, that we're dealing here with cultivated people who thought that,
helped by their literacy, they could achieve all sorts of things, even very
much. Once I walked along a road that was garlanded with wild flowers,
all was still, in the air and on the earth, and since everything solitary is
still and everything flowerlike and flowering may conjure feelings of
solitude, and since every plant reminds us of eternity and its tragedy, it
was no surprise that the heroism should come over me, and for a time I
believed I was a *Landsknecht*, a soldier of fortune, hastening boldly into
the distance, toward an absolutely unknown fate. Perhaps, on that occasion, lisping in this tree or that, this or that solitary leaf was unwittingly,
inconspicuously, and wonderfully illustrating the meaning of existence,
and now I doubtless make an unquestionably lovely assertion, if not

perhaps even a grand one, the drift of which would permit me to say that from the clouds, which resembled curiously huge couches and resting places, gods and goddesses at their repose gazed down upon this desolation of a landscape. Many landscapes, I must and without demur can say, have, whenever I walked toward them, embraced me, welcomed me, smiled at me, and with their lovely life set me in order. It was frivolous and rather irresponsible of me, on excursions and so forth, to have been able to imagine myself spontaneously a solid existence that nothing could rattle or shake, and that I knew what served me, what I could do, what I wanted, and that, to make me happy, here at my disposal was, for instance, a cigar, which I employed quite importantly, and almost never, facing such a landscape, did something frolicsome and witty occur to me, as if I didn't need anything like that, as if that wasn't beautiful enough for the person who, as he gazed, felt around him an ocean of air. I remember—and quite honestly believe that very, very few now understood me—I remember, so I say with a modest impertinence, that whenever I walked across an old wooden bridge, stood at the gate to a park, had before me a plateau, looked at a prospect, tried to assess, to treasure the twilight of a morning or evening, I had only earnest thoughts about myself and humankind, about being and the realm of stars, but strange, as soon as I resolved to write, happinesses flitted around me, it was as if writing appeared comical to me, and it may be in this way that I kept to myself much that was earnest. Moreover I make with pleasure the confession—which perhaps characterizes me—that while writing I might have been silent about rather much, quite unintentionally, too, for as a writer I preferred to speak not of what could be irksome, or difficult to express, but of lightness, whereas into what has occupied me here I did open out, with all the heaviness in me, though fugitively, of course, as seems to be my wont.

Probably Spring 1927. *B* 5.

Loud expressions of opinion

Loud expressions of opinion and confessions of faith seem to fall back into the mouths and throats of those who proclaim them. My head now light, now heavy as a lump of iron, I was walking along accompanied by many flying, floating, fluttering persuasions that, like annoyances, would not let me be, as if they fancied themselves too valuable to quit the alcoves of my peculiar self, toward something like a fairground, which made me at once forget that my chief executive's collar might just make me look a bit bizarre, which it probably did. Because I was afraid I might explode, that's to say, fall down in a maidenly faint, otherwise called a swoon, probably there was spread across my face a frightening sort of expression. Because I saw a high school teacher, who'd spotted me in the turmoil of people, lunge suddenly toward a pretty bourgeoise, on his lips the shout "Do please take care of yourself with that man around," my decidedly tenuous shape adopted measures even more precautionary. The face of the widow's protector looked pallid as the snow. Meanwhile with heartening clarity I saw my thoughts rear up in me like snakes, as if they intended to consume my friends, who might now be my enemies. I'd completely forgotten, among other things, my love affair with the tragedienne, which seemed comical to me, because she loved me and at the same time considered me a total washout, denizen of an era that seemed grand on the stage but only small in life, and who made upon herself perhaps the same impression. My hat being larger than my head might have increased the oddity of my appearance, and why, on top of it all, should I now, as I wandered not so very disoriented along life's path, be thinking of the poet Novalis so intensely that I felt a person of importance approaching me barely noticed, who now put to me the quiet question: "Why do you disguise yourself really?" "My disguise can be due to my being sensitive to yourself" was the answer I gave, with a modesty almost intimidating, bewildering, having as example a quite definite type of modesty in my mind's eye, which lent my gaze perhaps a nonchalant, dreamy air, as if I lay promenading around in a sumptuous yet lacerated bed. The person briefly said farewell and slowly walked away, leaving me the impression that she'd been prey to a certain indignation, and now the moon music, the moonbeam maiden, the moonshine chamber came back to my mind, and with these notions the night through which stormed and echoed the ravishing calls of enthusiastic songbirds, and which I'd spent with her at a window and knew no way to converse but by holding both her hands, who now had approached me on the fairground. A weary literary world-celebrity rode with the most exquisite bearing high on a horse through the midst of the motley crowd, melancholily tolerating this district of the everyday. A fragrance of cakes freshly baking stole into innumerable noses, and the idea that I, too, was endowed with a nose restored to me the courage to grip the I that I'd multifariously denied and now allowed to say yes to itself. A series of green hills framed, as curls frame a beautiful face, the theater of the fairground, where was to be seen the calf with more legs than nature usually admitted. Earnest and significant buildings peeped from a distance, as if approving of the frivolity, down into the joys of the circus, which might only have been set up so that all the participants had no obligation but to know as little as possible about each other, to seek no more kindness of heart than they themselves perhaps possessed. If a strong man had ample energy to distinguish him, a feelingless idiot received from assailants, who derided the pleasure they took in aggression, punches as bold as they were unfelt, and whereas some soared in carriages, others exercised themselves in aiming and delivering promptly shots in the shooting gallery. Those who yearned for adventure sought to shed some signs of that by endeavoring to exhibit orderly faces. The naif and inexperienced instinctively assumed an aspect of worldly wiseness. Schoolboys, children, mothers, maidservants seemed never to tire of craving for pleasure and of despising their joys like old maids who know too well that dainty lovelocks have long gone out of fashion. I was afraid I might meet the high school teacher again, who was doubtless also timorously thinking he might have occasion to obtain more respect from me than before. O, the sky, floating over the scene, what a beautiful song it caroled, and you yourself, darling, twittered and whispered so sweetly once in a theater-box, which, like a luxury gondola, cradled you, for all around you my delighted, pious devotion flew and made me most solicitously stay far away from you for years on end. What will your earnest heart say to this dutifully merry-mooded letter, in which, as in a bluish-black pond are mirrored the jagged peaks of a heart's mountain and the fir trees of a yearning to scale myself, to view again my steadfastnesses, though there's no reason to suppose I wouldn't like to see you, wouldn't like you to catch a glimpse of me.

Probably Spring–Summer 1927. *B* 4.

Letter to a Patient Lady

My colleagues, perhaps not all but probably many of them, work sometimes through the night, whereas for ages I haven't been able to do so. Today, dear lady, I tell you by lamplight that for a fairly long time, about a year and a half, I have had a ladylove, and at the same time I tell you of a very peculiar circumstance, namely, that my bed moved strangely last night, as if it meant to reach up over me, envelop and crush me, and nobody was doing this but solely and uniquely she whom I love.

As regards this love for a ladylove, I only notice something of it when I'm feeling somehow unwell, when a distress, a sick feeling, rears up before me. Every time something incomprehensible strikes me and plunges me into thought, then she emerges to stand right there in front of me in all her perpendicular and slender impertinence; for that is it, she is impertinent, by which I mean to say that I consider her colossally uneducated.

For a while she wore velvet slippers, exactly as you once did; she also has the same first name, and it's as if she has borrowed her equanimity from you, too, the slight lassitude of heart, this small, sweetest, cosy, fair amount of indifference with which some women of the lower classes see that they are luckily provided. Moreover, I don't know if I still love her today; that's something never known precisely, I think, nor is it necessary to know it. But I'll write to you in another way about it. The manner in which I'm confiding in you here might be rather offensive to you. Now I notice it.

You were being compared with someone of whom I've begun to speak as if I despised her, which implies that I don't have a high opinion of you. And then this bed, which rebelled against me. How will you understand that? The bed went quiet; but then it seemed as if my hands wanted to fall off. All of a sudden these hands of mine were creatures with a will of their own, and as such they wanted to walk off somewhere into the night, and when I checked their movement, they started to cry like discontented, small, sick children who are upset because tired.

Can you imagine that? Afterwards I fell into a deep sleep. Every so often I have, by the way, something like an epileptic fit, and the turbulent bed might be connected with what I mention. Recently I had a sort of fever, but if I now confess to you, most esteemed lady, that at night I sometimes have the sensation that my hands and feet are crumbling, decaying, as if they were being vaporized, dissolving; if I add that at such moments I am almost turning, in a peculiar but also simple manner, into dust, mortar, earth, and that I feel this with great clarity, then you will find that I'm coming up with something weird.

And now again this bed reaching upward, which incidentally did become well behaved and sensible again, and my ladylove who only seems to be there, really there, when death looms huge. O what a jolly letter I thought I was going to write to you, and now it has turned out to be a deeply thoughtful one, so reflective and frosty as to be almost genteel.

I lay there awake and hadn't the slightest aversion to myself or to anyone else, nor did I feel the slightest needle-thin bit afraid of myself or of my surroundings, or of the idea of the world, an idea so flattering yet so harmful. I'm usually well again in the mornings. If you saw my ladylove you might be inclined to call her a mediocrity. She writes poems and lives beside a lake, and once she pushed a defensive fist against the breast of an older suitor.

And so now I've hurt your feelings, but just think how I hurt hers, whom once I addressed with endearments, think how she has hurt his feelings, who is now writing to you, it's a long bothersome and yet entirely botherless story. How beautiful the face of existence was yesterday, the grass yellow, on the path there were felled treetrunks, and a colleague of mine got married in a mountain village. Will he write works of lasting merit there? I cut for myself a hazelwood stick, so that I might hold in my hand something that resembled a whip, thus to make me look like Beardsley's Mademoiselle Maupin. There are two kinds of writer, the ones who write as fluently, pointlessly, and plentifully as they talk in society, and those who are, when they write, quite different from when they converse.

I sent you some newspaper clippings, so that you'd see I'm active. Hands that tend to cross over into the other world are truly dubious adherents.— I hope I'll sleep better tonight. She knows, too, precisely how long you've been my altogether kind and considerate friend. If only I never saw her again! That wish will enable you to judge what she means to me; she means more to me than you, I dare tell you as much because you have a heart for me; she has none, and has it always been the case that people with heart are aflame for the heartless, and did this always turn out to be quite natural?

Will the people who are not important always be having a quiet significance and the important people wanting what that contains?

May 1927: Prager Presse. SW 18.

The stage-space might have measured

The stage-space might have measured twenty meters in height, producing the impression of an overwhelming Will to Culture. Of myself I can attest most humbly that at an age of about eleven I stood as dancing master there on the podium, which was smooth as glass. Earlier, much earlier even, yes, in fact it may have been thirty-two years that were attributed to me. But now I was radiant, sparkling, before me something entirely new to my experience. I was young, indescribably so, and whom did I have before me but the adult, beautiful Preziosa, who, face to face with my sense of responsibility, which directed me to train this superlative embodiment of joie de vivre, quivered in all her wondrous and seemingly chiseled or molded limbs. As no one will find cause to doubt, her costume consisted of lightsomeness itself. Unknown though her origin might be, she was so strikingly like a Swiss that anyone would have had the greatest difficulty in declaring that she was not. To that extent she had a native country of excellent landscapes, and her not being lax, not questioning anything but her task, this I took care of, in expectation that she would perform leaps two meters high, although, should the need arise, double that elasticity and agility was hers to display. It was my main duty to appear to be keeping in reserve any likelihood that she could ever gratify me. My dancing-master instincts provided that, to this being before me, whom I truly worshiped, I presented a face and an attitude across which crowded, as in a stormy springtime gale, flashes of contempt. Never should she come to feel that any ineptitude of hers was not, to me, unforgivable. Nevertheless her technique bordered on the fabulous and when gradually she came to resemble an angel in paradise, apparently shedding all gravity, materiality, necessitudes, and hankerings, when in the context of her profession she behaved like a shuttlecock being played with by happy people on a summer holiday, transients in a region where all was delight and frolic, then for this welcome situation, this enchanting reality, she thanked naturally me alone and the merciful mercilessnesses to which for her benefit I had roused myself, whereas I'd have preferred to caress her, to tease her with spiteful requests as to propriety, or, speaking with a little more refinement, to harass and certainly bore her a bit. During rehearsals she'd turn, with a plea that I quietly found most amusing, to people who were present, not uninfluential people, indeed respected persons with an interest in the arts, that they should tell me to be a little more tolerant of her; but this achieved nothing, except that, with a condescending smile perhaps, she'd be advised to continue respecting her *instructeur*, for she had, after all, entrusted herself to me, and, as she might see, if I deserved it in every way, then they were justified. Several sensitive women, whose gracious figures bestowed upon the box where they sat the look, somewhat, of a painting, might find from time to time that I was all too principled, but that gave them not the slightest reason to withhold their applause, which I valued, and which I perceived as a mark of attention, though not one to be overestimated, since gratitude too vehemently emphasized is in effect indiscreet. For the sympathy accorded my endeavors I thanked them by heaping upon Preziosa entirely haphazard, thus unwarranted, reproofs, certainly a most peculiar compensatory measure, which raised audible laughs. I heard them lisp: She is heavenly, and in fact it was gracious, I'd like to believe grand, of her to permit herself to be fascinated by a figure of stature as puny as I myself. What mattered was learning and absorbing, not the stature, imposing or not, of the educator and teacher—that was a watchword of mine. How well he knows the way to subdue her, one could hear them say. Perhaps nobody but I understood how, straining every nerve of her being, she might be animated by the conviction that I loved her and would fain be nothing but her servant, and that all my bouts of impatience signified only homage. To my nonchalance I joined an inexhaustible zeal, and if I gave her an education, I had a right to do so, because from the start I sensed that she demanded it of me, and for that reason was, without any long deliberation over the matter, happy. Education is always a reciprocal affair, the teachers learn from those they teach, who learn from them. And came the day when I did make her triumph, make her a person perhaps not completely, but still, in her own way, happy, by allowing myself a mood, a lapse, I don't know what, in which, for once intimidated, despairing, I looked up to her, not because of her mastery, but because of a feeling, which I could not resist, nor did I wish to, that she was a mensch.

1927. *B* 4.

Looking out into the landscape

Looking out into the landscape, I'm able to observe that what moves can appear more graceful, more beautiful, more noble that what stands firm or is stable. For just now, simply and evidently because they are stable, the trees and saplings are being shaken by the wind. Now and then, insofar as they yield, they are shaken. If they weren't rooted, there'd be no rustling of their leaves, and consequently no listening. The listening depends on the rustling, the rustling on the shaking, the shaking on the fixity of the objects, which grow out of a definite place. The fugitive masses of cloud, beautiful, grandiose, don't stand firm, and so evince no shaking. Entire mountains and fortresses of cloud seem almost indolent, like swans swimming along or women being disposed to smile or to move. The disposition of what is beautiful, soft, and eminent, peaks in a totality of quiet compliance, as is the case, for instance, with acts of kindness, with justice, with love. Inaudible, without a murmur, when blown upon by the primeval mouth of the wind, the grandest comprehension dissipates. Tranquil and persistent phenomena which resist that vital force, or offer to resist it, are meanwhile there, incomprehensible as well as comprehensible, and in a most delicious way they seem to know and to complement one another.

Summer—Autumn 1927. *B* 5.

It's still not so long ago

It's still not so long ago that I had an urge sometimes to roar. A rage, directed mainly against myself, turned my inner life into a quivering phosphoric bog. My estimable intestines were dancing, crying out loud, by which I really mean that I behaved as usual. Bandits pitched their somber tent in me, and in such a manner of speaking I discern above all a certain open-heartedness, which surely deserves due recognition. I've altogether stopped speaking of snakes and suchlike. Might I be downright wrong about myself, believing myself transformed into a tiger, for instance, which, claws frantically gripping its victim, glass eyes gazing deep into the unthinkable, gradually retreats from its cruelty? Moreover I'm convinced that this tiger longs to shake off its existence, to be something more beautiful than the terror that clings to its image. Are we all, actually, mere images for our highly esteemed fellow-men? Sometimes that seems to me so, and all of a sudden I'll speak now of an uncanny figure, a sort of criminalist, who approached me last night in his actor's tinsel overcoat, at a fairly early hour. He was smoking a *Stumpen,* one of those short cigars with a heavy narcotizing aroma, and his gait seemed to me like a subtle, satanic smile, at the same time noble and vulgar. With this very cultivated person, who is to all appearances more of a furtive conspirator than an official emissary, I once took afternoon tea in a splendid apartment; out of politeness it was offered to me, and one can call it a literary tea, because the two of us spoke of nothing but literary curiosities, and it was the occasion on which suddenly he aimed at me a searching look, as if he were putting a quite particular question that was incredibly important to him. Nervously letting fall, with charming urbanity, a passing mention of some long-ruined Roman cities in Africa, as seems to be the custom at such bellelettristic entertainments, he revealed to me that he considered himself a solitary person, and this for the almost laughable reason that others thought him so. "I have murdered," the phrase slid among others from his mouth, as if what he was saying overmastered him and the master was to be obeyed. I didn't jump out of my chair, no, not at all, but thought it fit to reply, in the quietest manner, that he had certainly murdered several times over, without ever taking account of it, and that he now persuaded himself he was a murderer because, to his regret, it wasn't at all true: that he had a mighty craving for vitality and imagined now and then that he lived with a charming woman, who had been poisoned by his iniquities. A stab of pain seemed to pass through him, and after a pause he said: "What a devil you are, to disallow me the illusion that I'm the person you strip off me." Moreover his tea was rather watery, and with a certainly somewhat unpleasant somnolence I announced that I was in love with the mother of a very beautiful school mistress. Beauty, I explained in terms theoretical and apparently tested by practice, induces the unbeautiful, just as pure conservatism induces subversion. "You venture to speak of politics?" "In my opinion nothing is not political. Everything, beginning with this scoop I lift from the carefully polished floor, is political. Every step, every kiss, every gift, every word, every mouthful of food, every hat, every pair of trousers, every breath drawn belongs with politics, and that's a fact of which I'm unshakeably convinced." "Do you mean to deny," he asked me earnestly, "that you are a child?" "I know that I can be terrible," I replied, and benevolently, that is, airily, I added: "For instance, I find it most appropriate that with praise one can undermine, but with undercutting cavil one can be enlivening, uplifting, and all these many clever aberrations, these dark-edged brilliancies, these foolish understandings, I find them terribly interesting, actually enchanting at times. If I go in search, for instance, as a seeker, I never find anything. By the way, do you know that I have a patroness who thinks herself neglected by me, and spurned?" There are more misunderstandings in life than there are stones on the ground—I snipped the thread, which he picked up and spun further by remarking: "Once or twice I've seen you down below my hilly domain, boyishly throwing stones, which does set you in a certain light." "To a person displaced, not to say vegetating, outside the frame of society, I did once make a shattering proposal with regard to the well-being of her soul, which can be doubtless viewed as an adjunct to my foible for gallantry." That concluded the tea, and I know full well that we are inimical friends, two who attempt reciprocally to catch one another out, two enthusiastic fanatics of honor, for whom it is a joy to be under no obligation to have too excellent an opinion of one another, whereby each of us endeavors to consider his adversary much too intelligent to be just, such being the desire of persons who are somewhat decadent, which is how each, for decency's sake, considers the other, no other possibility of being at all moral showing itself. "So the rascal has two houses!" Thus do I, with my many lodgings, exclaim in cold dismay. What concern is it of his, this evangelical Catholic, this powdered touslehead, this buttoned-up nude, this prissy man, rhapsodist of nobility and kitchenmaids, this idealistic cynic, this messy-minded martinet, this life-affirming monster of negation, this unimaginably polite miscreant, et cetera, that I'm sometimes under the illusion of being a bit of a boy; after all, one of my loveliest duties is to keep myself going, because I serve the God of Goodness as his dwelling place, though sometimes I only have straw for him to rest his limbs on. Don't I, too, love the supreme being? What does he really mean, coming at me with this appellation enfant terrible? In certain articles he's good at launching to propose that each day I pass along a certain architectonically valuable alley because my vileness draws me there, whereas it's a plain fact that thereabouts I hope to meet with troops of lost children. More specifically, it's there that novellas, so to speak, are alive and float unwritten, all ready-made, between those walls. As for him, my opponent, the only possible subject is laughed to scorn by nice girls he finds congenial. They laugh him to scorn because they find him kindly and because they realize he doesn't understand it, the dummy. Also he doesn't know that, like walls, the hours close in on us, that I am in several ways a gravedigger. He thinks I had an eye on his spouse, because she spoke to me once with feminine condescension. My abysses are utterly alien to him. He thought he could annihilate me, and here I am, his annihilator, at which he can only rejoice, for it is the haters, the killers who make us brace ourselves, as waves make us love life and welcome it with extraordinary freshness, when with desirous arms they embrace us and breathe into us the flowering sense of dissolution. He's nothing but a circumspect, calculating philistine.

September 1927. B 4.

Cabaret Scene

The Impresario
Your career, do you want to ruin it?

The Flapper
Once and for all,
Get this: my name is Flapper. Now
What a dismal face you're making. Me,
A pleasure person is what I am.
Enamored of joy. So I say little of it.
Say it, and you lose it. Ho hum,
Lady Muck, I think it was, the other day,
Honored me with her attentions.

Impresario
Any moment now, and here she comes,
Andalusia!

Flapper
A pretty dance,
Considering she has the toothache.

A Lady Typist
Flapper has talent, no doubt about it.
I tried to make a person of her once,
Someone sensible, I mean, someone
Dependable. My good intentions met
Head on with her belief
That she's just fine the way she is.

Impresario
There was a time I called her Fräulein Doktor.
She's a decent sort, I am inclined to say.
I seldom saw such a lavish spender.

Flapper

Ever since you discerned in me
An inner life, mister,
You've gone great guns to put me down.

Typist

No imagination. If the kid had some
She'd think I was a countess.

A Society Woman

When she speaks to me, as if it were
Unutterably natural, she presumes
To use the familiar form of address.

Impresario

Sir, I must advise you
That Andalusia is, to all appearances,
Beset by certain fantasies:
She thinks you are her father.

A Schoolboy

Well, it's a fib.

Impresario

O be mute! This is a serious matter.
(*To Flapper*) Order at once for Andalusia
A bottle of champagne. That'll pacify her.
She's very cross.

Flapper

Here she comes. I'll be bound,
She looks like a snowstorm in that outfit.
Not a whiff of the industrial zone
About her. A dancer, O
The moment I set eyes on one
I feel I'm a baron. The feeling
Must be congenital. My father spent
Ten years in Paris during the Second Empire.
The sights he saw. Constantin Guys
Fixed them on paper, magically,
With a crayon of genius.

A Teacher

Of the real world

That Flapper has no conception.

When I tried to slip her one, I only ended up

Wanting her to find me rather charming.

Society Woman

Flapper, just the person to bring to me

A letter on a silver salver, and a thrill

When I open it.

Only look at her, and life seems rosy.

Her face, her demeanor, it's music.

Flapper

That nurse in the hospital,

Whenever she walked away

I thumbed my nose at her. Stockings,

She wore white cotton stockings.

Impresario

Convince Andalusia, you must,

That you're crazy about her. Do it,

And I won't call you a barbarian. I promise.

Flapper

How beautiful they are,

Women who fight their wounded feelings down.

The brilliance of her eyes quite turns me on.

White as alabaster her complexion now.

I am inspired to be dauntless! I can't help it,

Her act has fortified my faith in myself.

The beauty of an artiste, what is it for,

If not to strengthen and enrich the soul?

Schoolboy

She's got a gun.

Impresario

She's taking aim.

Society Woman

Who at? Ah, interesting.

Andalusia
(*shoots*)

Flapper
(*slightly wounded*)
Merci beaucoup.

Teacher
Poor dear.
(*Flapper is bandaged, looks thus much to her advantage*)

Flapper
Andalusia, you are a nervous wreck.
(*Adopts the posture of a dreamy shepherdess*)
O the goddesses,
Feathers in their hair, clothed
In the absolute of clotheslessness,
Call it nudity, if you must,
And who approach you as you stop,
A captive of thought,
In the solitary green
Ocean of leaves in a forest . . . Impresario?
Order up the bottle you mentioned. Now.

Impresario
You're on the track to reality at last.

Flapper
And glasses for everyone.

Society Woman
Who'll ever find this sketch
Believable? Sobersided readers
Might not applaud it,
Though they should.

Flapper
How deeply moving still they are, the pains
Flaubert took while writing. His zeal,
His strenuous self-discipline. It's almost
The stuff of fairytales.

                    People do make sense
Calling me a literary dude. For
In so-called realistic books reality begins
To look unreal. Our urge
To be alive is opposed by life itself.
And reality is subtle, life is subtle,
What's more we can create reality
Insofar as it does consist of ourselves.
And since we are educable, then
So-called reality must be educable, too.
Whether it's poor or rich is up to us,
So as a meaningful factor,
Even as a decisive one, I bring
The unreal into the orbit of the real
As its proper complement.
                         You do not see,
For instance, shadows in the sunshine.
And if I were to lose reality, if it became
That much more real because I search for it,
What then? Isn't the searching
Just as real as the little reality
I have and am?

Impresario
Prost, prof.

October 1927. SW 17.

The idea was a delicate one

The idea was a delicate one. So he approached the difficulty of it like a breath, quietly. He was supposed to write something about the garden outside the window of his writing room: "The garden on my mind is beautiful because it is loving and fragrant. Everywhere in a garden one encounters love, replete with hanging plants." Might that so be said? How delicate it was again, this question, in which everything looked like morning and evening at the same time. Didn't flowers look at him as if with questioning eyes, and didn't their light appear both familiar and strange to him, ages old and never there? Whenever he stopped to think, didn't he resemble a flower that kissed itself in the exercise of its patience? Something that perceived itself, like a breath of wind, flew in at the window, and, like a child, was felt to be there, only unseen. Every garden has something naif about it, and his was no exception. Actually no garden wishes to be more beautiful than another, for gardens love one another, or so at least one thinks. A nature subtilized as one can perhaps call it, its trees are special ones, so are its leaves, which seem to have been educated somewhere. I won't stop outside its frame, I'll stay, gladly linger, in the decoration of its edges, which are affable, for it is pleasant there, in the daytime as by night. The branches, the stalks, are remarkable, swaying, hushing, also in their speaking suppleness, and indeed how singular are the roots, in their dark existence, which, like the holiness of light, is the stuff of fairytales. Adjacent garden huts, with which people complete their gardens, are civil as a smile, for they serve at most for social coffee drinking or the solitary writing of poems, depending on the occupant of this kind of structure. A garden is easily adapted for garden parties, at which arrangements of musical creations come into play and a sufficiency of artificial lighting into use. If one so desires, if one allows oneself as much, one can learn all sorts of things from the flowers. They have incomparable grace and are friends without equal,

92

fresh and gentle, carefree and humble, and they raise no objection to being smelled, or else they behave as if this were not forbidden; they are pious without knowing anything of piety, good without knowing anything of goodness, and they love nothing. Is that perhaps why one loves them so much? They look out, as if an enthusiasm enveloped them. For them one is enthused, everlastingly enthused as they are, seeming to derive from the age called golden by some solitary people. Once there was a person whom two women loved without ever being the least bit vexed at one another, unavoidable as that might otherwise, in such a case, have seemed. These two women made an excellent name for themselves in history. They were a rarity, and certainly they fit into my little description for today, which I hope will meet your wishes.

Spring 1928. *B* 5.

Execution Story

Owing to an attic apartment he was inconceivably young, and an uncommonly nice woman, who now and then offered him a bonbon, seduced him into writing a book people described as terrifying because it took no account of the gravity of the times. Because the book was madly funny, it was pronounced a product of madness, and while reading it the not unrespected daughter of a bourgeois family fell lifeless to the floor, having actually died laughing at what was in it. Painfully educated young men, at the sight of its concoction, aghast at its dumbfounding untendentiousness, melted clean away, so breathless that they went all to pieces. A friend of his once had occasion to tell him that he would achieve inconsequential successes and, in consequence of his successful inconsequence, people inviting him to afternoon tea would at the same time opine that he must be terminated. Those pronouncements were now to be borne out, for masked men, with a dry command to accompany them, walked into his shimmering jewel of a room. Since the duty of these persons was to secure his being thus accompanied, they arrested him, and while leaving the place in which he'd brought, through the opening that he'd come to believe was his mouth, many a cake, he theatrically exclaimed: "I'll not see thee again!"

A court of literature, as ruthlessly composed as any ever, snarled him to death, whereupon a lady who heard the proceedings hastened to explain that she wanted to appoint this manufacturer of such an utterly abject intellectual product as her husband.

The tribunalist judged her desire to be admissible. He was a bon vivant in whose eyes dying and marrying came to just about the same thing. What a lovely look in her eyes! However, when the object of her choice, believing at the decisive moment that he should be a complete man, refused, albeit with the utmost courtesy, the attractively tendered support, the person in question broke out into an "Aaahhh!" as if meaning to rejoice at her disappointment and lament the thwarting of her attempt to embrace him. Did it not look as if she loved him only now, just when it was of no avail to her?

In the gallery by that time handkerchiefs were held in readiness, the man condemned to die was dead in the soul now. His past life, already strange to him, eyed him like a faint light from far away.

"Conduct this sinner to a place where apparently no improprieties occur, with a promptitude sufficient to restore to the esteemed and interesting lady, whose emotional state I can understand, the composure to which, as I would not doubt for a moment, she is accustomed," said with positively splendid professional aplomb the principal of these proceedings in the Chamber, a command at which the beadles had no occasion to demur, and with which they complied without more ado.

The high-hearted lady, who seemed to be in need of some breathing exercises, was gently carried out into the amenities of the fresh air. At the wondrous sight, a casual passer-by most unforeseeably fell in love with her.

While the judge, in his in no wise unluxurious home, and beaming with satisfaction, settled at table to enjoy a gracefully served soup, the subtle silken evildoer enjoyed an excellent execution.

On the way to it he felt as light as fluff.

Perhaps an execution drawing by Rembrandt, which I saw at one time or another, justifies at most by the way this precious and derisible story.

Probably 1928. SW 20.

To a Poet

Why did you go, not long since, to those forever silent, satisfied ones who envelop their grandly frugal state in vestures of a signally tacit uniformity and can place their eloquence in a wave of the hand, who stand before their houses like images in bronze and told you by their bearing that you lacked something; why, when seeing yourself before them, whose etiquette is inimitable, did you hanker after the inconsequence of, for example, a little chat?

But first of all I'd like to ask you to tell me how it happens that in your mouth a crude expression cannot be crude at all: why you are unable to make your harmonies, which are certainly valuable in themselves, duly effective? Didn't you visit a night spot to see life pulsating, though you were not penetrated by it, for you knew it already, which is why I address to you the question: Wouldn't you have preferred to be lifted into life knowing somewhat less?

When you arrived among the aforementioned figures, did you already understand them all too precisely, so that they could never be an experience for you? As a child you were like a sonata in the form of a model, perhaps unprecedented, of intuition. Perhaps you always remained a precocious boy, and this if anything chiefly because you were never able to be witty, wit being a liberty one endeavors to overcome, not a distinction for which one craves.

There accompanied you always an innate earnestness, not one you'd labored to acquire, but one that you received, it might be said, as a gift, an earnestness you gladly wore like an expensive article of clothing. Constantly your surrounding world had occasion to revere you; on this esteem you walked as on a carpet, so your feet did not come now and then into contact with a country road, such as might have told you stories of all sorts. You moved continuously in a society in the face of which you never once needed to be all of a dither, which even turned itself into a zither on whose strings you nonchalantly played. Nobody smiled at you other than kindly and politely, so you, too, never smiled other than courteously, and you became accustomed to a differentiatedness, which was reflected on those who perceived in you this refinement, seeing it as a kind of beauty.

Cities and landscapes you experienced, and you did not experience them, because the illusion of them had surrounded you at the age of nine. Did you not forbid yourself certain skills, on the grounds that they were not in good taste? Why did something attract you to the inimitably delicate, who are able to lament for their lives without batting an eyelid, to whom you seemed no stranger, as you believed you noticed in their monotonous behavior, and to whom belongs the art of being indulgent as well as a sight to be seen.

You tried to be laconic as a stone in a quiet place and frisky as a rivulet, and your restraint was converted into a dalliance, and your speaking did not speak, and one voice turned on you her back, because toward her you behaved as if she were not worthy to be met, the voice that compels belief.

July 1928: *Individualität. SW* 19.

She addressed me in the formal style

She addressed me in the formal style as no one else would have dared to do, I know. I also know that while conversing with me she played at being silly, being a nitwit. Some arbitrary nitwit stood before me, stiff and straight as a candle or lamppost, and, hands propped on supple hips, snapped at me. Sillier, more mindless stuff had never been garbled or nuzzled together. Uniquely she, who claimed to be descended from an interesting person, seems to have had the ability to diminutivize me, with a noisy swish and a swing. It was no pleasure, no gratification, to have to do with a schoolboy who thinks he's numero uno in the knowledge of life, she said, ridiculing me, and she seemed to be perfectly right, and all this time I was sitting there actually touched, imagining to myself that such righteousness was an effrontery. Since she knew me as someone gentle, who made concessions, it was no extravagant audacity on her part to treat me so roughly. In the way I gave her time to unburden her heart to me, to vilify me thoroughly, I found amusement, treated myself richly to it, for everyone is honestly eager to have fun and unequivocally enjoy himself. Joys that one is constrained to doubt, more or less, are everywhere to be had. "You, a lion? Yes, perhaps from a distance, but close up more like a mouse, or some tip of a lappet." While she talked at me she didn't look at me, not at all; she said what she had to say as to a public, for the generality, and the effect was therefore as entertaining as it was objective. It goes without saying that she came up once more, as she did indeed often, with the boyishness, the naughty boy thing. She was behaving like a card-player's triumphant trump and I didn't utter a word to ask of her that she should allow for my peculiarity, et cetera, and should be considerate regarding my possible idiosyncracies. "Shut up! Not a word out of you!" Thus she'd rather mischievously dominate me from time to time, as if I'd protested, flared up, defended myself, which was absolutely not the case. Yet the fact was, she meant to be comical, she enjoyed her own drollery, and when incidentally she revealed to me: "You are utterly worthless, can't be considered a villager or a recognizable urbanite," she had no purpose but to laugh at herself and at her convictions as to my laughable traits. But in her zeal to seem earnest she entirely forgot this last, because she had no time for it, and nor did I, because I was so stunned that I could only sit there in amazement. Since when have amazed people laughed and since when have laughing people been amazed, and since when do players of games not play to the exclusion of all else, and do speakers and listeners achieve anything besides speaking and listening, disregarding all else, neglecting all else? To take care of a lot of things at the same time isn't easy. Doing something presupposes desisting from something else you've completed or begun to do, and at root her abuse was something like a proof of her satisfaction with me, yet satisfaction with someone brings no satiety to soul and mind, and repose is glad to renew itself in restlessness. Besides, I was myself the one who spoke to me. I sat and stood at the same time, hushed and spoke and formed two persons from my own alone. It was, wasn't it, as if with the greatest levity and astonishing velocity thinkable one stood up from where one sat to stand speaking to the person one was a moment before and now no longer was, and yet remained that person still, because one is seeing oneself in imagination, which enriches life, which I employ as often as I want or can or may, which throws me off balance and always restores it, which is the continuous emotion for the sake of which I always and never go too far, which, as today for instance, multiplies me or at least doubles me now and then, which is strange and is pleasurable and keeps me active and therefore rejuvenated and foolish, so that one can experience being pleasured alive, so that it won't be all too self-evident, and not too lonesome, either.

August–September 1928. *B* 5.

Prose Piece

Between snowflakes and leaves there are resemblances. At the sight of snow falling one thinks that one is seeing small flowers that are falling from the sky. Why is foliage dying in the autumn secretly golden, and why does one think of springtime flowers having tongues, to shape some kind of conversation? Seeing leaves one thinks of hands, their finger-inesses are budlike. Birds' feathers, leaves on a tree, the delicate, feathery, fingery snowfall in winter—one rightly tells oneself that they are related. The wind seems to be an undependable blunderer; its lull is as sweet as compliance, blissful in itself, flowing round itself, feeling itself beautiful. Does the wind feel that it is windy? Does the leaf know how beautiful it is? Do the snowflakes smile and do flowers charm themselves, and do curls know their curliness? A river in its motion resembles a limber wanderer in a hurry, the watery mass of a lake in its repose a beautiful woman in white gloves, with blue eyes. The profusion of leaves hides the enchanting finery of the branches. It is a pretty thought that pretty things exist. The shapes of waves and branches are snaky, and times do come when one knows that one is no more and no less than waves and snow-flakes, or, as it certainly longs now and then for release from its uncommonly graceful confines, the leaf.

1927–28, possibly January 1929. *SW* 19.

My Endeavors

In the course of time I have become a cause for disquiet among my publishers. One of them once invited me to write a novella for him; but to this day I haven't managed to write a single novella. When I was twenty I wrote verse, and at the age of forty-eight I suddenly began to write verse again. In this present attempt at self-portraiture I will avoid, on principle, becoming personal. I won't be saying the least thing, for instance, about important personalities I've met during the course of my life. On the other hand, I'll talk as precisely as I can about my endeavors. Supposedly I have some reputation today as a writer of short stories. Perhaps the literary esteem in which little stories are held is relatively short-lived. May I also ask the reader, cordially, to rest assured that my utterances in these lines spring from good feeling? This moment is pleasant for me, I sense that I am a model of contentment. Till now, I've always written with composure, even though as a person I had the capacity to be restless. Incidentally, for about five years I've had a ladylove, for whom my love is not perhaps of the best quality. I read French now and then, but frankly I won't claim that I've understood, word for word, the books written in that language. With books as with people I consider complete understanding to be somewhat uninteresting, rather than productive. From time to time I perhaps allowed my reading to influence me. About twenty years ago I wrote, with some agility, three novels, which are possibly not novels at all but books in which all sorts of things are narrated and whose contents appear to be appreciated by a small circle of persons, or a large one. Some time ago a younger contemporary started a sort of quarrel with me, because I wasn't profoundly struck when it occurred to him to tell me that he revered this or that earlier book from my pen. But it's a fact that the work in question can hardly be found in a single bookshop, so its author really cannot be delighted. Perhaps it's the same for some of my esteemed colleagues. When I was at school, one of my educators, or teachers, praised my handwriting, which in all likelihood is markedly a handwriting for prose pieces; it helped me to issue numerous sketches, et cetera, and enabled me to uphold my profession as a writer, for which I am of course glad. I crossed over in the past from book-composition to prose-piece writing because huge epic connections had begun, as it were, to get on my nerves. My hand became a sort of refusenik. In order to relieve it, I exacted from it only the supply of smaller testimonies, and behold, with suchlike deference, I gradually won it over again. Bridling my ambition, I instructed myself to be content with modest little successes. The writer inside me hearkened to the regulation of a person who wished quietly to go on living, who then had to deal with a variety of newspaper editors. Once I did have a better name, so I believe; yet I also have accommodated myself to a less distinguished one, desirous as I have been to declare myself agreeable to the designation "newspaper writer." Never was I adversely affected by the idea that people might think I'd gone artistically astray. The question "What you're doing isn't art any more, is it?" sometimes seemed to lay a hand gently on my shoulder. Yet I could tell myself that a person who persists in his endeavors did not need to be troubled by demands so laden with idealism that they made him miserable. I freely admit that I had no heart to deny myself the taking of a walk, within certain limits. For me it's enough to allow myself to think that time continued wondrously to look after me. I'm still alive and am thankful for that, and perhaps I may permissibly give thanks that I'm of a mind to be of one mind with myself. If I sometimes wrote at a venture, on impulse, it looked a bit comical to deadly earnest people; but I was experimenting with language, hoping that it contains an unknown livingness, the arousal of which is a joy. Insofar as I wished to enlarge my scope and made that wish come true, people may now and then have disapproved. Criticism will always keep company with endeavors.

1928–29. SW 20.

I Was Reading Two Stories

In a country house, or actually a little home in the country, I was divert-ing myself with a story that seemed none too complicated. On the roof, which reached almost to the flowers and herbs that covered the ground, a nightingale sang to please itself, something not meant for people averse to hearing it on account of its being too poetical.

While for my pleasure I was reading how a woman of refinement, a model of cultivation, in demi-colleté, I mean with polite deliberation exposing to view her pretty bust, suddenly thought of something that had slipped her mind for a moment, a wagon halted outside the house and two horses attached to it stood there as motionless as two brass, or bronze, or marble statues.

These animals are, depend on it, entirely fortuitous, insofar as I might just as well have had some other object position or display itself there. The road was wet, the meadows were shimmering. The trees—nut, apple, and others—stood like toys stuck in the ground by a child.

In appropriately slow motion a cow came past. Meanwhile, I was still preoccupied with the woman, who in her evening gown looked as if she were clad in an elegant, expensive, smiling, so to speak whispering, sack. Like bees from the beautifully shaped openings of flowers in a garden, remarkable little remarks flew from her charming little mouth. One might not be disinclined to characterize as "brilliant" the company in which she was sitting. All the more brilliant was what the young woman suddenly told herself: "I was forgetting the fix my mother is in." For her mother was, in fact, in a financial quandary. What a common utterance, in the midst of that literary, cultural, and artistic circle, yet to some extent it was not unwelcome, indeed it was just beautiful. The woman of refinement radiated an aroma of satisfaction to have brought a matter of urgency into consideration. She rejoiced at her dutiful punctilio, and standing up she announced: "I must quickly see to something, and knowing as I do that I am unexpendable, I must ask the present company to allow me the thought that the gap I leave behind me will be pleasing."

What she said was not so very astonishing, for she had a heart, and from that region spring the abilities that lend value to conduct.

The next day, while the leaves of surrounding trees, for all the world like scraps of paper, were looking in, one after another, at the window, taking up, tranquilly as a hermit might, or a teacher for once in the role of a pupil, a new story, I responded to it with emotion I could compare to a room with various people coming in and going out.

There was a girl who lived in a mountain village frequented by strangers, and she allowed into her soul, to reside and rule there, a foreigner. When, along with his excellent suiting, plus an alpenstock and mountain-conquering kit, he upped and awayed, she found she was unable to forget him. She couldn't help thinking of his features, incessantly, thus all the time, and of his little hat, which sat merrily and dependably on his head. He had told her of illustrious writers, artists, and statesmen, and the innocent little mountain girl, unable to pay due attention to his enthusiastic manner of speaking, devoted to his slender and intelligent figure the delicacy and immediacy of her remembrance, as it said yea to his many merits. He'd gone, like a scurrying squirrel, a ship swimming into the distance, or a flying affiliate of the bird-world.

With their coverlets of green velvet the mountains now looked all forlorn to her, the very shapes of sorrow. Back and forth she walked, as if life had no meaning for her. When she had carefully confided in her best friend, the latter wagged at her, to raise her spirits, a fan of words: "Don't lose hope."

August 1930. *SW* 20.

A Propos the Kissing of a Hand

Is it possible? Am I really capable of it? Yes, it seems so. One day I was delighted by a story. Since then I've read it several times. I've never forgotten it. I happily returned to it again and again.

Here now I'll report on its contents; it all happened in a house of quality.

What interested me transpired far away from any farming. As one got into the story, not one cowbell was to be heard. On characters and milieu there lay a breath of the city.

Splendid scenes would occur in a finely wallpapered salon. Doors were always being opened and neatly closed. Servants airily asked if so-and-so might be admitted. If admission was permitted, a fop or dandy would hurtle in, elegant and impulsive, approach the lady, who sat in a chair, and kiss her hand.

Most of the action apparently entailed officers. Officerly necks were stuck in high collars, legs in gleaming polished boots. Their speech glittered with chivalry and gallantry. Hair was at the same time barbered and tousled, in homage to naturalness as well as culture.

Ears hearkened, teeth showed behind lips. The writer had hold of a tempo in which steady regularity was combined with all sorts of quirks.

Every so often one of the women would politely recall that good manners were necessary and tact pleasing.

A tempestuous person could hardly be bridled. From time to time he'd be jumping out of his skin, that's to say, beside himself. To soothe him, the lover gave him her hand to kiss.

This movement she made with a wonderful grace. On her arms there shone and shimmered a bracelet, which seemed to be a world in itself. The hand was fragrant. There seemed to be relationships between her mouth and it. Now and then a little slippered foot would capriciously curl, perhaps to insinuate something.

Minor characters were mingled into the doings of the active ones. A little bunch of flowers, growing from a vase and standing on a table, told how lovely it was in the country, where one could effortlessly cope with contestable things, restless things.

Down below, carriages drew up at the portal with precision and noise, and from them somebody would dismount, someone in a hurry to climb out and rush up the staircase.

"Who might it be?" was asked in whispers. Again it was none but he at whom, with ample cause, one and all must tremble.

He was young, handsome, and exuberant, she sly and sensitive. Classicism in person, she had something fond and obstreperous to deal with in him.

On the water of the pond that appertained to the garden extending behind the house, swans were swimming.

He was always wanting more from her than she had the capacity to give, and again and again she found occasion to bid him content himself with kissing a small hand. Whereat her tender cheek took on a heavenly beautiful color.

There was a long wait.

1930–31. *SW* 20.

The Avenue

Probably the painter didn't see everything that I (for instance) did. I'm a poet, you know. I write verses, but not while nature is there immediately in front of me or while the poetic mood is on me; I save that up for later, pocket my impressions, things I've seen, and make off with the swag. It is a kind of code for conduct, I might say, a regulation; to that extent I'm a regulator, someone who stamps, whenever I press my stamp on ideas I've collected and, sensuously speaking, place them on file in a drawer. One day I saw a painter, with whom, incidentally, I'd exchanged only a word or two, casual words, polite words, a painter sitting with his equipment before a landscape and trying to capture it in an image. I only glanced at his drawing. It was just before lunch and first I had to ask myself what might be on the menu. Frankly, this was the question uppermost in my mind, and looking at the painter's work as something peripheral I saw there his strokes—strokes are props. Then at table there was fish, tasting quite splendid. As for the sauce served with it, even today, long after it was consumed, I can simply do no better than rejoice over it. Its quality was divine.

Whether the painter had seen this gem of an avenue I discovered one day thereabouts, whether to him it was vouchsafed to penetrate the thicket, the confusion of the landscape, seemed to me doubtful, because he was a married man. Husbands seldom flit far from their spouses, that's for sure. While the painter's wife was knitting a sock perhaps, or just darning one, he was making strokes, and this work of strokes was honest work, too. He seemed to be a good slipper-fancier, and now there passed over the lake an exceptionally windy wind. It was a regular whirl-wind racing over the clear, blue, beautiful, jubilant, bouncing, amiable, good water. The little trees on the shore had to stoop before this utterly dependable wind and seemingly were glad to be doing so. The wind silvered their shimmer, and now the painter sat there endeavoring to paint, with strokes, the wind, the waves, the entire glorious, passionate event, this phenomenon, and I saw at once that he lacked the requisite script, technique so-called. The wind was a white invisible thing, thus, no less, an invisible white thing. Of course, the invisible can be painted as it reflects itself on things that are evident.

So it appeared that this painter, him, hadn't discovered the uniquely beautiful avenue that I had discovered, and naturally I was glad of this, because it made the avenue something like my own special domain. It took me an hour to walk from one end of it to the other. So it was about four kilometers long and followed the line of the lake shore; and it was astonishingly, daintily beautiful, of an unspeakably sweet, mysterious sveltness, such as made it at home with itself in the air, like an adorable child seeing itself in a mirror that tells it how good it looks, something it is really better never to know. At himself nobody should look, for the loveliest and kindest mirror is love, and, by the way, it is in our related-nesses and loyalties that our reflections are their most vivifying and best. The avenue was of willow trees, some of which might be a century old, and perhaps the painter didn't see any bit of it, this wealth of magic in a landscape. It was a landscape exquisite beyond compare. In this pro-longed avenue one was quite overcome, so singular was it, so beautifully haloed and touched around with the gold of sundown; the beauty of it even made one a bit frightened. The avenue turned me into a diffident little boy—whether that's possible or not. The lake and the entire world, this high dome where all things are, stood calm and still, no noise, no breeze passed by, it was like song, it was like a gentle, solemn, joyful song worshiping creation, in beauty indescribable, and I'm trying here to convey it, as the painter tried to deal with the lake raked by the wind while I passed with my thoughts of lunch, with baked-fish thoughts and thoughts of lettuce, glancing at his apparently honest efforts.

Possibly his wife swept and dusted him quite a bit. It's wiser not to be saying much on that account. O, the avenue that I saw, opening itself to me, to me. When I entered it, I reveled in it. The grassy ground was green velvet, so yielding that you wanted to roll on it, all the lovely stuff seemed so untouched. For a long time, apparently, nobody had found any reason to go there. Now I'm here and it is there.

January 1931. *SW* 20.

Heroic Landscape

Only a few paths, faintly marked or furrowed, led through the landscape afloat in my mind's eye, one that interests me, which I would like to fashion into something of interest. Scant human figures were to be seen, and they seldom saw each other. Like loosened hair, which seemed to flutter everywhere, which could and would not be bound, the leaf-masses of trees moving back and forth spoke a language suited to the people, who uttered few words, who, taciturn, did think much. In earlier times there seems to have been more thought than is the case, for example, nowadays, when manners of speaking chivy thoughts away and hyperactivity has become a subtle and polite foe to thought, which latter wants to exist for its own sake, like a sky or an ocean; which one does not freshen up; and to which, by subjugating it to uses, one is not being useful.

The freely scattered crags, in their quiet, robust, austere beauty, looked like lovers of the trees, which loved the stormy wind that played with them. The rocks apparently failed to understand this, so the trees, which want to be seen in their fragile delicacy, spurned them. Massive things that cannot be toppled love thus, often, unrequitedly, and what roars along, exuberant and lusting to destroy, is what is loved. Slopes adorned with oaks, and impressive, arched high into the air, which was regarded as the Begetter of understanding between people, who were sometimes on the move, sometimes settling down. The dwellings, as they emerged, were still modest, still meek. Trade and industry were in their early, chaste, and charming stage, though sometimes those who practiced them thought their concerns were ancient; for ages there have been illusions about this.

At the doors of their carefully tidied huts, bearded bards reached venerable hands into the strings and sang of times gone by, when sons knew nothing of disobedience and daughters could infuse their parents' hearts with joy. "Always the same old song," they said, in a friendly way, to those who listened. At all times it has been lamented that lamentation is easy to understand, the reason being that it does touch us and teach us.

The same goes for me as I tell this. The heroic landscape seems more meaningful than the visible one around me, the present one, which is not eloquent enough, where the water cannot remotely compete with that which aforetimes was peopled by nixes, and at which, because it does not murmur and whisper secretly and puzzlingly, the possessor of Historical Connections can do no better than shrug.

Probably 1931–32. SW 20.

The Gifted Person

Into the Bahnhofstrasse spilled the vesperal fluid, whispering traffic. Athletes decorated with laurel wreaths that shimmered gold and silver in the torchlight were just then returning from the hubbub of a distant festival, to their wives and children who awaited their homecoming with impatience.

In an alley, conceivably almost romantic with its utter hush and sequesteredness, a woman, who felt at this instant beautiful, good, noble, magnanimous, and distinguished, was looking up at a room on the fourth or fifth floor, where from a window an incalculable young man, who suffered from mood swings, looked down upon her, and with a theatrical gesture threw to the timorous shadowy figure waiting there a rose, which he might have picked, unsolicited, with a lilylike tenderness, in a park. Wife though she was of a diamond merchant, she'd been promptly thrilled to have given her heart to somebody without any income to dispose of. He, however, seemed in his thoughts to be elsewhere, not with her, suffer as she might for him and his frolicsome spates of indifference. Let us leave her to her whispers, speaking to the rose she has received from his white hands, which glowed in the dark of night, words of endearment.

Being gifted he certainly deserved the reverences of a woman so sensitive and not at all unbeautiful, but divinely graceful and knowledgeable. The outstretch of her cultivation resembled an unsurveyable sea, and while he gaily and frivolously wrangled with himself, all those treasures lay at his feet.

Down the star-clouded alley a girl came leaping with an exclamation on her tongue: "Where shall I find the fellow who chatted me up for a while today and enchanted me, while so doing, with his lovelocks? I don't think I'll be able to endure life unless he shares it with me."

The woman, who seemed to nose out who it was that the newcomer was referring to in words that harmonized with the splash of fountains and the fragrance of flowers that issued from the local gardens, laughed at the tearful simpleton and spoke: "I am a heroine."

Said a passer-by: "For all my generally recognized capabilities and the respect I enjoy, I have never been loved."

The gifted person called down to the group: "Being touched by the sympathy shown me, as I live at the foot of the mountain, in the strange industrial city, where for a while the Italianist Gobineau sojourned once, my thoughts are upon the ravishing Jewess with whom, while a cloudburst was pouring down, I rode across the Potsdamer Platz in an omnibus."

c. 1932. SW 20.

The Lake

With every step on the way to the lake you look forward to the moment when first you see it. It is strange to imagine how it will look. An avenue of tall trees casting shadows leads to it, and it becomes gradually visible. All along the avenue, in gardens, there are buildings of many kinds, for example the dainty property of a prosperous spinster. A few steps on, there is the villa of a respected clock-maker, whose ingenuity and model dependability have earned him the good reputation he enjoys. I forgot to mention a museum, which appears winningly and not unimpressively at a point where the avenue forks left and right. In this house, which is not actually large, but which gives an impression of elegance, you can see, besides a variety of old pictures, conspicuous coins from bygone times, a number of spears, too, from a historic battlefield. Swimming in visibility there's a stuffed fish, and an unreal horseman, bearded, wearing a cloak, is riding along. Further on in the avenue your attention is caught by a fine house, fairly old, open for visits, to be reached via the little bridge that crosses a splashing stream. To this classical sort of a building a panel is attached, a memorial to the life of a strong character, a marked personality. A hospital façade is visible, and a country house from the pigtail era peeks out in its vicinity, so rococo. Now I've arrived at the lake shore and the beauty of it brings a smile to my heart. What a liberal distance, what a rich, clear space spreads out before me; my modest mouth can hardly indicate it, let alone describe it. It would take a poet to show, in appropriate and convincing words, what the eye encompasses, what it is that quickens the feelings. The lake lies there, untroubled, like a body in repose. If a wind went over it, there'd be waves. But since this is not so, it is like a mirror or a piece of silk stretched taut. It's morning, and now I walk, slowly or quickly, past a tennis court, likewise past a quarry. Alongside the road, which clings like a ribbon to the shore, run railway lines that shimmer in the sun enticingly. Delicate flowers wreathe the water's edge. Accompanying the lake, close to the road, rises a line of hills. Up to a certain level grow vines crisscrossed by little pathways. If I wanted, and if I had the time, I could now venture on, to walk round the lake, which would require ten or twelve hours of effort. Then I might happen to enter this tavern or that, not romantically but nicely, I mean idyllically situated, with a patio, and pass half an hour over a glass of wine. The fragrance of grapes growing by the lake reaches me from far off, and the wine, when new, is sweet, naturally losing its tastiness when it ages. It might be the same with human faculties. It is during youth that achievements occur. As the years pass, some of our faculties quit us, slip away, which is really not surprising. As for villages round the lake, there could be twenty of them. One of these brownish-colored villages possesses, in its church, high up on the slope, a gem of Gothic architecture, with windows enlivening the walls and a spire which cheerfully stands for faith. Of this Christian work of art several scholars have sung the praises, and published them in the Sunday papers. O, what a blessing, to be buried in this small, sweet churchyard, so one might exclaim, peremptorily, that the living might find the dead man's grave a thing of beauty. A walk round the lake would give me one further occasion, to discover a castle, where in medieval times a count lived, who commanded respect, who strode solemnly about, and whose spouse fully deserved to be called a pearl of womanhood. While he stood, or sat, in one of the numerous rooms in the castle, plunged deep in negotiations with a motley crowd of persons seeking his help, and weighed necessities, initiating affairs and helping them on, she walked in summery apparel around in the park, back and forth, reveling in her pretty appearance, which she knew was a sight worthwhile. The field was being ploughed; artisans were busy in the little town with their daily professional occupations. The bells, which could only be heard ringing on Sundays, kept their silence. In the forest, which bordered upon the castle, a huntsman peered attentively this way and that.

I am, for now, content with this essay.

July 1932: *Neue Zürcher Zeitung. SW* 20.

EPILOGUE

She who wears the long gloves,
Have you seen her ever?
The passion you began with.
All at once it's over.

Spread in time around you
A prospect full of laughter:
Taking fright it disappeared.
Has she never found you?

She took a mood quite early
To make on me her mark;
Everywhere was clarity
Till she left me in the dark.

The lady, whom one does not love,
As long as there were people
Swung up to reach a height,
She never leaves them quite.

    1930; *SW* 13 (poem "Kennst Du sie?").

NOTES

Brentano and *Brentano (III)*. Clemens Brentano (1778–1842) was of the second generation of Romantic poets. His famous collection (with Achim von Arnim) of folk-poems, *Des Knaben Wunderhorn*, has sometimes diverted attention from his own radiantly exuberant (and satirical) stories. Between 1902 and 1926, Walser (W. hereafter) wrote four texts about him. The long, verbless noun-phrase sequences of "Brentano (III)" mimic Brentano's own surges of lyric parataxis. Bettina was his sister, who later in life wrote enthusiastic letters to Goethe.

The Back Alley. The English title warps somewhat the original "Die Untere Gasse." In a "back alley" there are no bookshops. The original is a topographical name assigned in relation to an upper lane, as in Zürich, descending to the river Limmat; there is the "Oberdorf" above the "Niederdorf." W.'s alley must be in Biel, and for him it is a site at which poor as well as better-off people go shopping. There is no class-conflict here, just a wish that gentility might mitigate misery.

The Story of the Prodigal Son. In place of "prodigal," the German says "lost." In the original there is some intermittent mimicry of the voices of literal-minded, parochial (even philosophizing) old codgers ("Jawohl" and repetitiousness), who overlook entirely the New Testament source of the parable (Luke 15) and its metaphor of grace.

Hercules/Odysseus/Theseus. In several microscripts of the mid- and later 1920s, W. questions Hellenizing as humbug, symptomatic of the inability of leading German writers to shed their moral myopia and confront actual everyday life. These three jokes are contemporary with Kafka's paradoxes on mythic subjects.

And now he was playing, alas, the piano. The text begins with a parodic recapitulation of a trashy novel (W. called it "Anlesung," acquired reading), and continues with a mocking recall of an episode excluded from W.'s novel *Geschwister Tanner* (1906). "Rumbelow" is "Niederer" in the original: "Spatz" means "sparrow." The spelling of the lady's name varies in the source. "Niederdorf" is the old riverside district of Zürich where W. lodged at intervals, 1896–1902.

Ramses II. The German misspelling of the name is retained. "Pastor Künzli" alludes to the herbalist Johann Künzle (1857–1954), whose influential work *Chrut und Unchrut* appeared in 1911.

Spanish Wine Hall. Two Gallicisms retain their French sense, "refüsiert" (meaning critically condemned, not refused by publishers) and "seriös" (meaning not serious but solemn). These mark the spearker as a rather supercilious homunculus of letters. Mired in a shabby scene (commerce, automatism), his only refuge is a reverie, amid scrapings of music, which founders among clichés. A sort of self-caricature, the text blends comedy and mania, but hardly with, say, Gogol's brio. It is contemporary with Russian sketches by Daniil Kharms (of whose high absurdisms W. cannot have known).

It can so happen that. January–May 1926 there was in Morocco a serious rebellion of the Rif-Kabyls under Abd el Krim. W. is writing (tongue in both cheeks?) a garrulous leader of sorts.

Letter of a European. From other texts of the same year it might be inferred that the unidentified addressee is a figure halfway between the "Edith" of several stories and a Genius of Europe (Anima? World-Soul?). The "little book" would be W.'s *Die Rose* (1925), in which the matter of "Edith" is addressed. Several microscripts show how incensed W. was at Thomas Mann for reviewing *Die Rose* as (imaginably) the work of a child: cf. "It's still not so long ago," September 1927.

Apparently not a cloud. The close: Even while improvising, W. finds himself, as one who loves his country, having to defend his attitude against chauvinists, and Calvinists (the "numbered" and "purified"). However flightily he spins into the subjective, the jocular, the oneiric, he does not forget the civil aspects of his writing. "Union:" the original confederation of eight independent Swiss districts in 1354.

The Red Thread. "Sped through the boudoirs" translates an abstruse coinage: "Gemächerflucht," which must refer back to the *Don Giovanni* allusion, while it Germanizes the French "courreur d'alcôves" (obsolete?) for "womanizer." The French itself had borrowed *alcôve* from Spanish *alcoba*, bedroom.

Loud expressions of opinion. The source has a doubtful reading at the start: "seem" or "seemed"? Echte and Morlang adopt "seem," so a general claim is made that expression overt and direct annuls itself, and what follows is an oblique scanning of a scene epitomizing ambivalence, simulation, and disguise. "Lovelocks" in the source are "Schmachtlöckchen," while the "old maids" are "schmachtende Tanten" (the pun is poor and not translatable, though the "Tanten," too, are subject to vanity in display).

Cabaret Scene. The translation is a loose versification of a prose original, and some liberties have been taken in the phrasing. W. was writing dramolets or minidramas long before the *Hörspiel* or radio play was instituted.

The idea was a delicate one. Impromptu, self-reflexive, and distinctly owlish, the microscript is quite different from the two feuilletons that W. extracted from it for the periodical *Sport im Bild.* He alludes at the close to the early medieval Graf von Gleichen.

Execution Story. At the end of paragraph 3, the verbs *jubeln* and *klagen* (rejoice, lament) might mock their counterparts in Rilke's tenth *Duino Elegy* and *Sonnets to Orpheus,* 1, 8 (1923). That W. appreciated the later Rilke is indicated by his poem "Rilke" (*SW* 13), which purports to have been written at Rilke's graveside in Raron.

To a Poet. W. might have had Albert Steffens in mind, the Swiss anthroposophist. However, the wording indicates that it was Hugo von Hofmannsthal (with his motif of *une vie antérieure,* or "Prä-Existenz"). There was sporadic correspondence between the two writers before 1910, and a meeting in Berlin is attested to; by the mid-1920s Hofmannsthal has become, for W., a foremost "posh" writer who turns his back, Hellenizingly or otherwise, on present times. Notwithstanding the reverential tone in which W. addresses his subject, he calls him neither *Lyriker* nor *Dichter,* but "Poet," which has in German a derogatory overtone. The opening lines suggest a funereal scene, but Hofmannsthal died on July 15, 1929, one year after this text was published. Since *Individualität* was an anthroposophist journal, W. might well have combined elements from both Steffens and Hofmannsthal.

A Propos the Kissing of a Hand. "Officerly" from *offizierlich,* a pun, since *zierlich* means "delicate." The text (like "And now he was playing, alas, the piano") belongs in an extensive family of sketches, also microscripts, in which W. retells stories he has read, or else invented, after scanning jacket illustrations of trashy novels. In one particular microscript, dated January–February, 1928, he defends trashy literature as an essential feature in literary tradition (*B* 5, 321–24).

The Gifted Person. "Bahnhofstrasse" is the main shopping street in Zürich. "Potsdamer Platz" is in central Berlin. The language of the source is singularly stiff, not so much marking, perhaps, W.'s malaise, as composed to show everyday characters in their isolation, with much to say, and craving drama, but whose speaking is so larded with cliché as to thwart communication.

A CHRONOLOGY

Acknowledgment is gratefully made to Robert Mächler's *Das Leben Robert Walsers* (1966) and to detailed chronologies in Robert Walser, *Leben und Werk* (1980), and in the volumes of *Sämtliche Werke* (for example, *Seeland*, Bd. 7, 1986); also to Werner Morlang's *Robert Walser in Bern* (1995), and to Bernard Echte's "Chronik von Leben und Werk" in *Du: Die Zeitschrift der Kultur* (Zürich), October 2002; most gratefully of all to Jochen Greven, but for whose congeniality, impeccable editing, and lifetime of unflagging dedication, Walser's life and writing might never have been well remembered.

BIEL (Central Switzerland): 1878–95

1878:   April 15, Robert Otto Walser born, the seventh of eight children.

1886–92:   primary and junior schools. Schooling ends due to family's straitened circumstances.

1892–95:   apprentice clerk at Berne Cantonal Bank in Biel.

1894:   October 22, death of mother, Elisa Walser-Marti.

1895:   one year in Stuttgart. Wishes to be an actor.

ZÜRICH: 1896–1905

1896:   various clerical jobs, changes of address.

1897:   end of November, visits Berlin

1898:   May 8, first publication, poems in J. V. Widmann's *Sonntagsblatt des Bunds* (Berne). Meets Franz Blei, essayist and bibliophile in Zürich.

1899:   end of January–Autumn in Thun. Works at a bank, at a brewery. First prose piece ("Der Greifensee") published in *Der Bund*: four poems in *Die Insel* (Munich). October, in Solothurn. Reads Jean Paul Richter's novel *Die Flegeljahre*.

1900:   in Solothurn until April. November 28, in Munich.

1901:   early January, returns to Switzerland. July, in Munich, meets the circle of young writers associated with the new review, *Die Insel*, where in September his verse dramolet "Schneewittchen" appears (later celebrated by Walter Benjamin). Mid-October, returns to Zürich, writes *Fritz Kochers Aufsätze*, and takes the manuscript to Berlin.

1902:   April, returns to Zürich, no publisher found. Clerical jobs (intermittent). March–June, in Winterthur, works in the Ganzoni elastic factory. *Die Insel* closes down.

1903:   military training in Berne. August–January 4, 1904, clerk to the engineer and inventor Carl Dubler in Wädenswil (near Zürich)—later the scene of the novel *Der Gehülfe*.

1904:   January–November, clerk at Zürich Cantonal Bank. Insel Verlag (Munich) publishes *Fritz Kochers Aufsätze* (with illustrations by brother, Karl Walser), in an edition of 1,200 copies.

BERLIN: 1905–13

1905:   March, sojourn with brother, Karl, who is already having success with stage-sets and book-illustration. October–December, servant at Schloss Dambrau in Upper Silesia.

1906:   January–February, writes first novel, *Geschwister Tanner* in Karl's apartment. Recommended by Christian Morgenstern, it is accepted by the publisher Bruno Cassirer. A second novel, in which the hero travels to Asia, is written, then lost or destroyed.

1907:   *Geschwister Tanner* appears (February). *Der Gehülfe* is completed (Bruno Cassirer, 1908). Rents a room of his own.

1908:   another novel, *Jakob von Gunten*, is written (Bruno Cassirer, Spring 1909). June or July: balloon journey to Königsberg with Paul Cassirer, art dealer.

1909:   *Gedichte* (poems) published by Cassirer in a bibliophile edition, with etchings by Karl Walser. *Jakob von Gunten* (no success) is read in Prague by Kafka, who gives a copy to Max Brod, such is his delectation.

1910:   employment perhaps, but brief, at the "Berliner Sezession," modern art gallery. Marriage of Karl. W. moves into a room between Charlottenburg and Spandau: "Dissolution all around me." Allegedly he smashes, at a party, the publisher Samuel Fischer's collection of Caruso phonograph records.

1911–12: Cassirer stops payment of advances. Another lean year, though two papers still publish his feuilletons. Kurt Wolff now contacts W., who assembles short prose texts for the books *Aufsätze* and *Geschichten* (1913, 1914).

1913:   March, returns to Switzerland; as from Summer, occupies for the next seven years an attic room in the (residential) hotel "Blaues Kreuz" in Biel. June, *Aufsätze* published by Kurt Wolff, also in the yearbook *Arkadia* three short prose texts (and Kafka's "Das Urteil"). Beginning of friendship and correspondence with Frieda Mermet, laundrywoman of Bellelay in Jura.

1914:   February 9, death of father, Adolf Walser. Prepares for Kurt Wolff the collection *Kleine Dichtungen*, which appears in the Autumn; W. is awarded a prize by "The Women's League to Honor Rhineland Poets" (2d impression, 1915). August 4: outbreak of First World War. Each year till 1918 W. now does, for weeks at a time, military service.

1915:   early January, to Leipzig for book signing (*Kleine Dichtungen*), with excursion to Berlin, visiting Karl.

1916:   writes *Der Spaziergang*. November 17, death of brother, Ernst, in Waldau Mental Hospital, where he had been since 1898.

1917:   publications: *Prosastücke* (Rascher Verlag, Zürich), *Der Spaziergang* (Huber Verlag, Frauenfeld), *Kleine Prosa*, (Francke Verlag, Biel). July 16–September 8: military service in the Tessin (Italian Switzerland).

1918:   *Poetenleben* (Huber Verlag).

1919:   May 1, suicide of brother, Hermann. A legacy of SF. 5000 comes to W. Publications: *Komödie* (four dramolets, Bruno Cassirer, Berlin); *Gedichte* (2d edition, Bruno Cassirer). Finishes the novel *Tobold*, of which only fragments survive.

1920:   November, W. walks from Biel to Zürich to give a reading from his newly published collection of longer prose, *Seeland* (illustrated by Karl Walser); at rehearsal it is insisted that the Hottingen Readers' Circle would prefer Hans Trog to read (an editor of the *Neue Zürcher Zeitung*); W. sits unobserved in the audience.

BERNE, 1921–29

During these years, there were at least fourteen changes of address.

1921:   his income from writing being so scant, W. accepts a post as assistant librarian in the Berne State Archives; after four months he quits, returning to his "short prose factory," that is, his desk.

1922:   March 8, reads (himself) to the Hottingen Readers' Circle from his new novel *Theodor* (finished November 1921), which is rejected by various publishers and eventually lost. Two weeks in March he spends at the home of the painter Ernst Morgenthaler at Wollishofen (Zürich), where he courts the 17-year-old maid, Hedwig. Attends a performance of *Fidelio*. Reads *The Brothers Karamazov*. Spring: inherits SF 10,000 from an uncle, Friedrich Walser-Hindermann.

1923:   June, hospitalized with sciatica. Autumn: a long walk from Berne to Geneva.

1924–25:   hereafter and into the early 1930s, frequent publication of feuilletons, sketches, improvisations, stories, in a dozen German periodicals and papers, also in the two German-language papers in Prague. Franz Hessel invites W. to contribute to *Vers und Prosa*, a stylish new periodical from Rowohlt Verlag (Berlin). The first "microscripts" are dated even earlier: minute and delicate calligraphy in pencil on the backs of calendars, rejection slips, scrap paper (etc.). The method spurred spontaneous improvisation, and was perhaps a mischievous symbolic rebuff to massive public demand for "reading material." Now he also writes poems again.

1925:   *Die Rose* (Rowohlt Verlag), his last short-prose book. Writes *Der Räuber*, a novel, in microscript, long believed lost, published in 1972. Begins correspondence with young Therese Breitbach (October)—among the microscripts there are many imaginary letters.

1928:   April 15, his fiftieth birthday. Prolific writing of prose and poems continues. Renewed depression: nightmares, aural hallucinations, exacerbation of troubles traceable to 1924–25.

WALDAU/HERISAU: 1929–56

1929:   January 24, at the urging of his always dependable sister Lisa (a schoolteacher), W. enters Waldau Mental Hospital, near Berne. He speaks of hearing voices. Keeps to himself, does routine tasks, gardening. Continues to write.

1930–32:   about thirty-five poems are published in *Prager Presse* and *Prager Tag-Blatt*, twice as many written but not submitted. Writes more than one hundred prose texts (quite apart from others editorially dated 1928–29), and not a few are published in German, Swiss, and Czech-German presses. He reads newspapers, completes crossword puzzles.

1933:   Contracts with Rascher Verlag for a new edition of *Geschwister Tanner*. June 19, is transferred, against his will, but in conformity with the law, to the mental hospital at Herisau in Canton Appenzell (W.'s canton of domicile). Lives quietly, does chores without demur, and institutional tasks, for example, making paper bags, sorting fruits and vegetables, twisting string, salvaging tinfoil from waste. Dapperly dressed, W. goes for walks in statutory free time, returns punctually, snow or shine. (Still in 1949 is documented as hearing [spiteful] voices.)

1936: the writer Carl Seelig visits him now and then; they go for walks together; during the next fifteen years, Seelig also sees to a few reprintings, for example, *Grosse Kleine Welt*, 1937, a selection.

1937–39: Seelig negotiates for W.'s release, but fails.

1943: death of Karl Walser.

1944: January, death of Lisa Walser. Spring: Seelig becomes W.'s legal guardian and executor. (May 1945: end of Second World War in Europe.)

1953: Helmut Kossodo Verlag (Geneva) publishes the first two volumes of a projected complete works, edited by Carl Seelig. (Later volumes were edited by Jochen Greven.)

1956: December 25, W. dies of a heart-attack while out for a walk.

1962: death of Carl Seelig in a street-car accident.

1966: first two volumes of a scholarly edition, edited by Jochen Greven (*Sämtliche Werke in einzelnen Bänden*, 1–20).

1973: Robert Walser Archive established in Zürich.

PREVIOUS TRANSLATIONS INTO ENGLISH

Walter Arndt

"For Zilch" and (two dramolets) "Cinderella" and "Snow White," in Mark Harman, ed., *Robert Walser Rediscovered* (see below).

Susan Bernofsky

Masquerade. Baltimore, Johns Hopkins University Press, 1990 (64 stories, 24 of them in collaboration with Tom Whalen).

In *Review of Contemporary Fiction* 12, no. 1, 1992, the following titles: "Maidservant Story," "There Was Once, to My Knowledge, a Poet," "Letter to Max Brod," "Snow," "Laughter," "The Park," "Mehlmann: A Fairy Tale," and "Letter to Lisa Walser." Also, ibid., in collaboration with Tom Whalen, "I Contemplated Pride and Love," and "Style."

The Robber (novel). Lincoln, The University of Nebraska Press, 2000.

"The Forest," in Whalen, *The Nimble and the Lazy* (see below).

Mark Harman

Ten stories and three poems in *Robert Walser Rediscovered*, ed. Mark Harman. Hanover, University Press of New England, 1985.

"The Child," in *Comparative Criticism* (Cambridge University Press), 1984.

"Green," in *Georgia Review* 45, no. 2 (1991).

"Well Then," in *Review of Contemporary Fiction* 12, no. 1 (1992).

Herbert L. Kaufmann

"The Seamstress" and "Disaster," in *Lyrik und Prosa* 7 (1974) (Buffalo NY)

James Kirkup

Three stories in *Atlas Anthology III*. London, 1985.

Christopher Middleton

The Walk and Other Stories. London, John Calder, 1957.

Jakob von Gunten (novel). Austin, The University of Texas Press, 1969; reprinted by Vintage Books, 1983, and by New York Review Books, 1999.

Selected Stories. New York, Farrar, Straus, 1983; also Vintage Books, 1983, and New York Review Books, 2002 (33 stories and 12 translations by others).

Prose and poems in *Fragments of Imaginary Landscapes: June Nelson and Robert Walser*, ed. Carin Kuoni. New York, Swiss Institute, 1994.

"A Painter's Life," in *Robert Walser and the Visual Arts*, ed. Tamara Evans. New York, CUNY Graduate School, 1996.

"Poems from the Microscripts" (12 poems, 1927–28), in *PN Review* (Manchester, UK) 140 (July–August 2001).

Harriett Watts

"The Little Berliner," in *Selected Stories* (see above).

Tom Whalen

11 stories (some in collaboration) in *Selected Stories* (see above).

The Nimble and the Lazy. Black River Falls (WI), Obscure Publications, 2000 (11 stories in collaboration with Annette Wiesner).

"Four Shorts" (with Annette Wiesner) in *Witness* 16, no. 1 (2002).

The Special Robert Walser issue of *Review of Contemporary Fiction* (1992) contains numerous important essays by Swiss, German, and Anglophone Walserians, also a searching introduction by Susan Bernofsky and Tom Whalen, and, also by Tom Whalen, a bibliography. For good measure, see Tom Whalen's essay "Beneficent Irrelevancies: Robert Walser and *The Robber*," in *The Hollins Critic* (Hollins University, Virginia) 40, no. 1 (2003).